Friends to die for

Friends
to
die
for

Jane Sughrue Giberga

Dial Books New York

Published by Dial Books
A Division of Penguin Books USA Inc.
375 Hudson Street
New York, New York 10014
Copyright © 1997 by Jane Sughrue Giberga
All rights reserved
Designed by Pamela Darcy
Printed in the U.S.A. on acid-free paper
First Edition
1 3 5 7 9 10 8 6 4 2

Library of Congress Cataloging in Publication Data
Giberga, Jane Sughrue.
Friends to die for / Jane Sughrue Giberga.
p.   cm.
Summary: Sixteen-year-old Cristina is forced to evaluate her
sophisticated world of elegant New York apartments,
private schools, and rich friends when a peer is murdered
after a party they both attended.
ISBN 0-8037-2094-7 (hardcover)
[1. Murder—Fiction.   2. Wealth—Fiction.
3. New York (N.Y.)—Fiction.   4. Mystery and detective stories.]
I. Title.   PZ7.G33924Fr   1997   [Fic]—dc20   96-32146   CIP   AC

For Ulises,
Susana, Peter, and Elena
with love

Friends to die for

I'm so pissed.

If I read one more piece in the newspaper about the murder, or see one more "in-depth" account on the local TV news, I'm going to run away from home. And they never get it right. They all say basically the same thing:

TEEN MURDERED AFTER WILD PARTY IN FIFTH AVENUE PALACE

Then they go on and on about our crowd and how spoiled rotten we all are, living in big city apartments, doing the club scene, going to the "best" schools. It never comes up that we're not *all* rich. It's never mentioned that the schools we go to are tops academically—tough to get into and tougher to stay in. These "journalists" who chase us to and from school like packs of wild dogs make us sound like druggies and slavering sex fiends. The facts don't seem to interest them.

The party was at Markie Hannigan's. Her parents were both out of town. Her mother had been in California for a month or so, and her dad went to Europe or somewhere on business. Markie's apartment *is* one of those upper east side New York City palaces with a million rooms, a huge entrance hall with black and white tiles on the floor, and trees in big ceramic tubs everywhere. The tiles make me feel like some kind of an automated chess piece, and the trees—the trees are amazing. I live a few blocks from Markie, farther uptown and way east, almost to the river. It's no palace, my mother grew up there, and we have a couple of little green plants in pots. No trees.

Brian was late picking me up because he had soccer practice, so things were rocking by the time we got there. I was excited, *flying* in fact, because I had finally maneuvered Brian McAllister into taking me out on an actual date. He's my older brother Alex's classmate and best friend, a fellow jock and a major hunk, and I've been trying to get his attention as somebody other than Alex's kid sister for ages. I'd almost bagged it, but suddenly he got easier and easier to talk to—we seemed to be into the same music lately—so when Markie pulled this party together, I went for it.

You could hear the music in the elevator before it reached Markie's floor, and the doorman eyed us warily, like should he call the police now or wait awhile? And he's known me forever. Markie and I have been in this all-girls school together since pre-K.

Walking in there was a trip. The din of voices trying to talk and laugh over the music, and the smog of smoke with its strong, sweet smell of pot, gave the whole place a weird feel, as if somebody'd moved one of the sleazier downtown dance clubs up here into Markie's beautiful apartment. There were at least two hundred people in the huge living room, and Reenie Dumont bounced out of the crowded dining room as though she were a cork popping from a champagne bottle.

"Crissy!" she shrieked at me. "Bri!" She draped herself around Brian and kissed him on the lips. He looked at me wildly, like Get Her Off Me.

"Hi, Reenie. Where's Markie?"

She shrugged and wandered toward the living room. "Haven't seen her."

Markie emerged from one of the side hallways looking flushed. "Cristina! I thought you weren't coming. Hi, Brian."

"A few of your dearest and closest," I teased.

"I don't know who half of 'em are! How does the word get around?"

There was a scream from the living room, followed by the sound of breaking glass. We shoved our way in, trailing Markie, and got quickly to the center of the room, where a big guy I'd never seen before wearing a T-shirt that read "Safe Sex Sucks" stood holding a broken beer bottle.

"C'mon," he mumbled, glaring at George Benson. I certainly knew George, probably for as long as I'd known Markie. George is a sweetie, everyone's friend, somebody you can always call if you need a date for something and you're between boyfriends, which I usually am. George is kind of a sloppy drunk, and he smiled stupidly at this guy with the beer bottle as though he'd just paid him a compliment. George was sprawled all over one of the Hannigans' beautiful white leather sofas, and I was pretty sure he couldn't have stood up on his own no matter who wanted him to.

"Who are you?" Markie confronted the guy with the beer bottle, stepping between him and George.

"Somebody should relieve him of that bottle," Brian murmured to me, keeping his eyes on the guy. Brian's pretty big, but he's not a fighter. He hates fights, in fact, and the severed neck of that beer bottle looked absolutely lethal.

"Who *are* you?" Markie rephrased it.

"Who wants to know?" the guy sneered.

"Your hostess," somebody said.

"It's her apartment," somebody else said.

The guy laughed, looking Markie up and down. She's a great girl with a pretty, round face that makes her look younger than sixteen, which is how old we both are, but she's a little pudgy. She'd rather eat than anything, and she has stick-thin, super-chic parents, so she's kind of hung up about it.

"You got a name, fatty?" the big guy said.

"Get out," Markie told him. "I don't know how you got in, but get out. Now." There is nothing wimpy about Markie.

"You gonna throw me out?" He waved the bottle close to her face.

Brian nearly knocked me down as he lunged for the guy. He tackled him, and the guy fell into the crowd surrounding him like a great tree, rigid and still powerful.

"Grab the bottle!" somebody yelled, and Jeff Lawlor and Timmy Waring got into it, each grabbing one of the guy's flailing arms. There was so much screaming, scuffling, rolling around bumping into chairs and tables, it was hard to follow. I only wanted to see where Brian was, but he was underneath the guy he'd tackled. A lamp went over and there was less light. And the music—pounding, pulsating, relentless—made it all worse somehow, like a soundtrack. Only the picture wouldn't go away. There was no way to turn it off.

One girl kept screaming and screaming. She was on the other side of the fight or I would have dealt with her myself. She was somebody I'd seen around, but I couldn't think of her name or anything, and she was off the wall. She was probably stoned, and this fracas had finally penetrated the haze of whatever she was on, so she was freaking out. Then someone else screamed, a very different scream, a response to what was going on. I looked again for Brian and saw blood. Everywhere. All over the big guy, his T-shirt, his face, his jeans, all over Jeff and Timmy. Brian was sitting up, but he wasn't moving. His eyes were wide open and he looked sort of surprised. I pushed my way over to him and knelt down beside him.

"Bri—"

He looked glad to see me, but he didn't smile. "I'm okay." He was clutching his upper arm and there was blood all over his sleeve. "I think it's—superficial."

"Somebody call the police!" somebody said.

"Are you crazy?" That was Markie. Calling the police would be like calling her parents. Wherever they were.

Jeff Lawlor was sitting on the big guy who'd started it all. Actually, he was bouncing off him, since the big guy was trying to hump him off his chest. Timmy and another boy had pinned his arms, so he wasn't going anywhere.

Markie was amazing. She kept grabbing people and assigning jobs. "Reenie, go to my room and get T-shirts, sweatshirts, whatever you can find in my drawers to replace all this bloody stuff. We can't let people leave here looking like this! Hurry up. Leslie, go to the big bathroom at the end of this hall. Just before you get there, you'll see a closet. Get bandages, gauze, peroxide, whatever's in there. Emily—"

I won't tell you what the big guy was saying. He was cursing his head off, although he seemed to be having some trouble breathing. Jeff Lawlor's almost as big, and he was sitting on the guy's chest with the calm of somebody who's completely comfortable. The heaving had stopped. The creep's stomach muscles had finally given out.

Markie looked back at the big guy as though she'd forgotten all about him. "How'd he get in here?" Then she noticed Brian. "Oh, my God, Bri! Where's that damn bottle?"

Somebody standing near the pyramid of bodies held it up. It was horribly bloody.

Brian swayed against me. His color was awful, and the hand he held against his arm was oozing with blood. I couldn't believe it. Our first twenty minutes as a couple, and he was slashed and bleeding.

Markie squatted down beside us. "Can you walk, Bri? You could lie down in the guest room. It's closest, and I think it's empty."

"I'm not sure."

"He needs a doctor, Markie. He probably should have stitches."

"I'll call Dr. Navri. He lives upstairs. My father got him his apartment, so he should come. Wait right there. Pull a chair up behind him, Cris, so he has something to lean on."

She was gone, and Reenie arrived with a pile of clothing, Leslie Quinn right behind her with bandages, cotton, a bottle of peroxide. Jeff stood up and looked gleeful as he ordered Timmy and his partner to sit the big guy up. It took the three of them to wrestle him out of his bloody T-shirt and into a sweatshirt that still had price tags attached. It was hooded, which struck me funny somehow. Jeff and the other two boys took turns changing their own spattered shirts, and when everyone in the group was finally pristine, they shoved the big guy toward the front door.

"I'm going," he growled, completely subdued by now. "I don't need a frigging escort."

"We wouldn't want you to lose your way," Jeff said, sneering and shoving him through the open doorway by keeping hold of one of his arms. "We realize how far you've wandered from your own part of town."

Everyone stood around watching as the elevator arrived and the three enforcers pushed the big guy on. The girl who had been freaking ran after them. I suddenly remembered her name: Janine Billings. She went to school around the corner from me, and she was supposed to be really wild. The elevator door slid shut and they were gone. Relief flooded the apartment like a breaking wave.

People were crowding around Brian now, and he looked gray. I tried not to panic. The music still blared. My head ached to the beat of it. The room had cleared considerably, and people were leaving in clusters. A large group was already out in the hallway waiting for the elevator.

Markie rushed back to us. "He's there and he's coming." She was obviously very relieved. "He says we'll probably have to take Brian to Lenox Hill, because if there's any stitching to do, he'll have to do it there. I'll call my father's car service."

Dr. Navri was a tall, skinny, handsome East Indian. He was calm and caring and told Brian he needed stitches.

"I'll call a car service," Markie repeated.

Dr. Navri looked at her quizzically, the slightest smile twitching his lips. "That won't be necessary, Marguerite. My car is right out front."

Markie was going to come with us, but I told her to stay with her guests and I'd call her when we got home.

"Bri—I'm so sorry." She was following us to the elevator.

"Forget it," Brian said. He had a navy blazer draped over his shoulders. He looked weak and unbelievably pale. I wondered whether the blazer belonged to Markie or her father. I didn't care. It covered the bloody sleeve, which was all that concerned her. Brian was all that concerned me.

"Call me!" was her last order as the elevator door closed and we started down.

I waited for over an hour at Lenox Hill. Dr. Navri swept Brian away, and I sat and worried. For over an hour. That's like forever, when you're worrying. I looked at the row of pay phones against one wall and thought of calling home, but they'd freak. *I* was freaking. What if he lost the use of his arm? What if there was brain damage from the loss of so much blood? What if . . .

I picked up a magazine. I didn't even glance at the cover, but I didn't have to look at it long to know I wasn't interested. When I did check out the cover, it read *Car and Driver*.

I thought about Markie's party and how she'd dreamed it up in school a couple of days ago. She'd had parties before when her parents were away. Her parents were always away. She bragged about what an expert she'd become at getting things repaired and cleaned and replaced.

I wondered whether there was any blood on the Aubusson carpet in the living room. Maybe something besides Brian had been slashed by that beer bottle, one of those gorgeous leather sofas, perhaps. That wouldn't be so easy to fix.

Her party, her problem. I thought about the others, the ones I knew who'd been there, who'd left so fast when things got out of hand. They were all dancing the night away at

Ferdy's or Centerstage or Bouncer's. No waiting on those endless lines outside on the sidewalk, either. The A List, our crowd. Strictly the A List.

I remembered now seeing Francesca and Gordon wander in after the fight. It hadn't really registered at the time, I was so frantic about Brian, but I wondered whether they were just arriving, or emerging from one of the six bedrooms in Markie's apartment. They looked pretty rumpled, so they'd probably been there awhile. Weird. I'd hardly noticed them, and Francesca is my closest friend in the world.

Actually, not when she is with Gordon.

Dr. Navri finally surfaced with Brian. The bloody shirt was gone, and Brian's arm was bandaged all the way from his shoulder to his elbow. He looked much better and he was smiling. Not his super smile that makes me weak in the knees, but a smile.

"Seven stitches," Dr. Navri reported. "No muscle damage, nothing severed. He'll have a small scar."

"I can't go to soccer practice for at least a week," Brian complained.

"I've given him a note for his coach," Dr. Navri said. "And I'll see you one week from today to take those stitches out, Brian. Have your parents call me."

"Yes, sir. Thank you, Dr. Navri."

Dr. Navri looked from Brian to me and shook his head.

"Thank you, Dr. Navri," I added.

"Take care, both of you. You've been very lucky, you know."

"We know. Thanks."

"I will never understand . . ." he said, and he turned away.

We got a cab fairly quickly. I gave the driver Brian's address.

"I should take you home first," he muttered.

"That's okay. You should get home, take it easy."

"It's only ten-thirty."

"I'll keep the cab, take myself home."

"Are you sure?"

I wasn't sure of anything. "Brian—"

"Don't worry about it, Crissy. It was dumb of me to do that."

"You were incredible! God only knows what that idiot would have done."

"Markie shouldn't give parties when her parents are away."

I looked at him in the semidarkness of the cab. Lights from the street splashed across his face like flickering images in a film. He is absolutely gorgeous, a hunk by anybody's standards, and he doesn't have a clue about it. He sensed me staring. He shifted slightly and sat up straighter, which must have made his arm hurt, because he groaned.

"Markie shouldn't give parties," he repeated, "unless—"

"She certainly can't give them when they *are* home."

"Why not?"

"You've never met her parents. They are two of the most high-powered people on the planet. Markie's been on her own since birth, practically."

"Well, she almost bought it tonight. That guy was a major sleaze."

"Are your parents going to go ballistic?"

"Naw. Well, my mom'll have a fit. My dad's cool. He'll

blame it on New York. He blames everything on New York. Then they'll start again about 'Why do we live here?' "

"Your mother was born here, like my mother."

"Which is why we live here. But my dad keeps talking about California, and my mother says everyone gets divorced in California."

"Everyone gets divorced in New York. Except our parents. Markie says the only reason her parents are still together is they're never in the same place at the same time."

We had arrived at Brian's apartment house, which is a couple of blocks from mine. He paid the cabbie and told him where to take me. He slid across to get out, then looked back at me. I had practically stopped breathing to keep from crying hysterically. He smiled, sort of, and slid part of the way back. And then he leaned over and kissed me. I could not believe it. It was gentle, it was quick, but he kissed me on the lips and then slid away again and was out of the cab in what looked like a single move. Athletes.

"Later," he said, sensing his doorman approaching.

I sobbed riding home. I mean, the pressure, the fright, the horror of the whole evening caved in on me, and I was a blubbering wreck. I felt marvelous.

It was twenty minutes to eleven as I rode up in my elevator, wondering what on earth to tell my parents. We're into the truth in a big way in my family, but I was already editing in my head.

Telling the truth did not mean telling them everything.

My mother just quit her job. Before that we were a normal American family: three kids, two incomes, five totally independent lives sharing one large, old-fashioned apartment on East Eighty-second Street in Manhattan.

I remember to this minute how much I hated it when my mother first went back to work full-time. I was twelve, my brother Alex was thirteen, and Mark was six and finally a first grader. She worked three days a week for a while, but she was such an instant success, she was soon working five days. My father said if he'd known what a business whiz he'd married, he'd have stayed home with us from the beginning and let *her* have the career. He was kidding, but I think he probably should have done that. He's much easier to deal with than Mom. I got over hating Mom's job very quickly. I've been absolutely in charge of my own life for too long to go back to having somebody hovering, monitoring my every move.

So I guess we're in the middle of a family crisis. I mean, aside from the fact that my little brother, Mark, was hit by a cab on Lexington Avenue. It *is* absolutely the worst thing that has ever happened to us, and we are all still vibrating. But I'm just not sure how we're going to cope with having Mom home full-time. I have to say I think she's overreacting.

Mark is fine—enjoying ill health, in fact, now that the worst of the pain and the scary part are over. He had to have surgery on one leg, it was so badly shattered, and he can't go back to school until after the Christmas holidays: doctor's orders. But the way he spins around this apartment on his crutches, they should make it an Olympic sport; he'd be a star. He's incredibly lazy about his physical therapy, though, and he totally cons Mrs. Wilbur, the home therapist who comes here three times a week to work with him, but Mom keeps after him. She's hyper about his doing everything the doctor prescribes, and then some.

It was so early when I got in from Markie's party, my parents knew something was up. They were in the den watching *A Room with a View* on the VCR for probably the fortieth time.

"Hi, gorgeous," my father said, pausing the tape.

"What's happened?" my mother wanted to know. Her Irish-English ancestry. The news is always going to be bad.

"Nothing." I flopped onto the sofa next to them, and Dad hugged me. He's into hugging. He still watches cartoons with us on Saturday mornings, although I don't get up that early much anymore. Alex and Mark do.

"Want to watch *A Room with a View*?" Dad gets a bigger kick out of movies at home with the family than the fancy business dinners and stuff he has to go to all the time. A fact. My mother complains about all the running around they do, but she's the scenester. Or was, before Mark's accident.

"Something must have happened," she said now. "Did you and Brian have a fight?"

"No."

"Why does there always have to be something wrong?"

my father asked her. "Maybe the party was dull. Maybe she's tired."

"Ed, she's sixteen."

The phone rang and it was Mrs. McAllister, Brian's mother. I squeezed my eyes shut as my mother groaned and uttered, "Oh, no! Oh, *no!*" a lot. I had had an Official Version of What Happened all worked out.

My mother hung up. My father had turned the TV and VCR completely off.

"Markie's parents are away, aren't they?" she asked me. When I nodded, she sighed and glanced around at my father, but she wasn't looking for anything from him. She always handles this sort of stuff on her own, and she lets him know when she wants him to get into it. "There was a terrible fight at Markie's party," she filled him in, eyeballing me as she spoke. "Brian had to subdue some big bully wielding a broken beer bottle, and he had to have seven stitches in his arm for his trouble."

My father has a short fuse. His face was blotching red.

"Who was this bully?" my mother asked me.

"Nobody knew him."

"Then what was he doing there? How did he happen to be there?"

"I don't know, Mom."

"Is Brian in the hospital?" My father.

"No."

"He's home." My mother cut me off. "He'll have to rest and take it easy for a week or so. Markie knew a doctor in the building, apparently. I would never have let you go if I'd known her parents were away."

"Mom—"

"Was anyone else hurt?" my father asked me.

"No."

"Don't sulk, young lady. Were the police called?"

"No, Daddy. It was all over very quickly."

"Brian could have been badly hurt," my mother said. "He could have been killed."

"Was this bully drunk? Stoned?"

"I'm not sure."

"Calm down, Ed," my mother told him. His face was now beet red. "You'd better get to bed, Cristina." She had eyeballed me again, but this time she was getting me out of there before my father blew sky-high.

"That's it for your party schedule," my father sputtered as I headed for my room. "You can do some studying for a change."

I slammed into my room and lit a cigarette. Terrific. Thank you so much, Mrs. McAllister. I should have gone dancing after I dropped Brian off. It might have been my last chance to party for some time to come.

You guys should have to deal. You have Wanda the Wimp for a daughter.

I made a decision when I was eleven not to do drugs. I had this friend, Naomi Crossman, who was getting wired every day, and I was alone with her in her apartment one afternoon when she freaked out completely. I had to call 911, and she ended up in a detox center. We were in seventh grade at the time.

I could tell you some horror stories.

I flicked on my CD player. I wasn't sure what disc I'd left

17.

in there, but I was glad to hear Sheryl Crow's easy sound. My room was thick with cigarette smoke when my mother knocked a couple of hours later. She came right in, of course. Privacy is just another empty word in our house. She waved more than she needed to at the smoky air and went directly to my window, which she pulled wide open. Then she came and sat on the end of my bed, where I had been sprawled staring into space and listening to music the whole time I'd been in there.

"Alex just got home," she said. "He and Kate ran into Francesca someplace, and she told them about Brian."

As I said, Brian is Alex's best friend. They're in the same class and they're the stars of the soccer team. Alex's girlfriend, Kate Lovett, is in my class, so it's weird we don't do more together, but Alex hates my party scene and most of my friends.

My brother Alex doesn't care about my mother being home all the time. He's so laid back he's almost invisible, and he's seventeen and a male. That helps—don't kid yourself.

Alex is totally straight. There's never been anyone as straight as him except maybe my father. He doesn't smoke or drink and he works out every day. I smoke cigarettes, *regular* cigarettes, and it drives him bananas. I'll take a drink too. I absolutely love the buzz you get from champagne, but I don't get the chance to have it very often.

Where on earth had they run into Francesca?

"He's terribly upset about it." My mother was pushing for a reaction from me.

"Does he want to talk?"

"Maybe tomorrow. He's gone to bed. There's some sort

of pickup game in Central Park tomorrow morning, so he's getting up very early."

See what I mean?

"Is there anything else we should know about all this, Cristina?"

"No, Mom."

"Did you know Markie's parents were away?"

I didn't say anything for a minute. "Markie's parents are always away."

"Then you don't go there for parties. You know that. It's not like it's a new rule or anything."

"I know, Mom."

"Remember David Ingersoll?"

I rolled my eyes. David Ingersoll was also in Alex's class. He'd had a big party when his parents were in Tokyo on a business trip. Everyone got stoned, the neighbors complained about the noise, the police raided the party, and David spent the night in jail. It finished his plans to go to law school, and his father's a big political type, so it was a very huge deal. I knew sometime during one of these Don't Ever Let This Happen Again lectures, David Ingersoll's downfall would come up.

"It can't have been fun, seeing Brian so badly hurt." My mother is relentless.

My eyes filled. I try never to cry in public, except during the sad parts of movies. Crying is such a ploy for so many people.

"Get to sleep." My mother'd gotten up and turned off my CD player. "It's a wonder you can breathe in here, with all this smoke."

She came over and brushed my forehead with her lips.

Mom's not nearly as demonstrative as Dad; all those repressed Irish Catholic genes, I guess.

"You can help me with some stuff tomorrow," she said. "Now that we don't have Miriam anymore and Mark to take care of, this apartment gets to be more than I can handle alone."

"I'm supposed to go to a yearbook meeting. At Leslie Quinn's."

"It must be the first one," she guessed correctly. She is always way ahead of me. "You'll have plenty of time to catch up."

She left then and I closed my window, lit another cigarette, and turned on a CD. I felt like a bug trapped in a bottle, and my mother had just tightened the lid.

Francesca called me the next morning. My mother had come in to tell me breakfast was ready. It was only ten o'clock, it was Sunday morning, I'd been sound asleep, and breakfast makes me barf.

Mom also opened my window again. Wide. She had just left the room, in fact, when the phone rang. There are four extensions in the apartment, and on weekends when the phone rings, four people often answer at the same time. My mother picked up in her bedroom, my father in the den, Alex in his room, and I in mine.

"Hi, all!" Francesca greeted us. She was used to this.

"Good morning, Francesca," my mother said.

"Hi," my father murmured.

"Okay," Alex said, hanging up. There was another click, undoubtedly my father, and then my mother said, "Don't talk too long, Cristina. Your eggs will get cold." And she hung up.

"Eggs?" Francesca was gagging on the word as I would gag on the eggs.

"Don't ask. Where'd you run into my brother?"

"We had been to Bouncer's, and he and Kate were coming from Cinema One. They do make a neat couple. They just don't look like they're from New York. More like tourists from Delaware or somewhere wonderfully *clean.*"

"I suppose everybody from Markie's went to Bouncer's."

"Nobody but us. Reenie was chattering about Ferdy's, going down in the elevator. How is Brian?"

"He had to have seven stitches in his arm."

"Ouch!" There was a pause. "Are we the only ones on the line?"

"Sure. Why?"

"You haven't heard obviously."

"Heard what?"

"Janine Billings was murdered."

"Janine Billings?"

"She came with Nicky Baylor."

"Who's Nicky Baylor?" I was beginning to wonder if we'd been at the same party.

"Cris! Honestly! Nicky Baylor's the guy who caused the fight last night. Brian got slashed. You do remember that."

I let it all sink in.

"Janine Billings came with Nicky. You've seen her around:

frumpy, dense. She trails after Nicky and Gordon like a stray cat."

"She was murdered?"

"Murdered."

"But—how? Who?"

"Her throat was cut. Who is not known, at this time."

"Where—?"

"It was on the late news last night. I always tape the eleven o'clock news and watch it when I finally get home. That way I don't miss anything. Imagine my surprise last night, when Janine's pudding face appeared—a yearbook portrait, undoubtedly—and the newscaster identified her and went on to say she'd been found in the subway in a pool of her own blood."

"Oh, my God!"

"They didn't say which subway station last night, but it's all over the papers and every newscast this morning. I'll bet you can guess."

"Eighty-sixth and Lexington?"

"Give that girl a free ride on the number six train!"

"Francesca—"

"There's been no mention of Markie or Markie's party. Maybe they won't make the connection."

"What connection?"

"She was found around nine-thirty."

"She was lying in a pool of her own blood at the Eighty-sixth Street subway station at nine-thirty? It's still really crowded around there at nine-thirty on a Saturday night. It's not possible for somebody to get murdered where there's a crowd!"

"It's totally possible, Cris. When was the last time you

saw anyone rush to the aid of anyone else in this town? Who even looks at anyone else in New York? It's amazing she wasn't left there for *days*."

"My parents will freak."

"Why would you tell them? Unless the police dig it up. Unless it gets out that the last place she was seen alive—"

"How do you know Markie's was the last place she was seen alive?"

"I don't know anything. I just can't believe it!"

I didn't know what to say. I kept seeing that hysterical girl standing rigidly still in the midst of all that chaos, screaming and screaming, completely out of control. And later, when the bully—Nicky Baylor, her date, apparently—had been shoved onto the elevator, she had run after him frantically, as if she were afraid to be left in hostile territory. And now she was dead. She was my age, maybe a little older. She went to school around the corner from me, and she lives— lived—on East Ninety-fourth Street. I knew exactly where she lived because there have been stories for a couple of years about Janine Billings and her apartment. She lived there with her mother, but her mother's never there, and if you and your boyfriend wanted to get it together some afternoon after school, Janine would provide you with a bed and complete privacy for a price.

"Cris? Are you there?"

"I'm here."

"It makes me wretched, just talking about it. Can you come over later?"

"I'm not sure. My mother needs me to help her here."

"You could say you were going to visit Brian. You could even *do* that, briefly, you're so allergic to fudging."

Fudging is Francesca's word for lying. She uses language freely, like a lot of other things, and the truth, she's told me a hundred times, is only for "reference, historical reference. Ultimately what is known about one must be factual, but in the interim, expediency rules."

I told her I'd call her back. I pulled on a robe and went into the den. It was empty, happily, and the morning paper was sprawled all over the room: first section on the desk, second section on the sofa, Book Review, Magazine section, and the mountainous rest of the Sunday *Times* strewn over every chair, table, and footstool in the room.

I found what I was looking for on the inside back page of the first section. The "yearbook portrait" Francesca had described stared back at me blandly, and a brief article on the discovery of the body in the subway followed.

"The victim was identified as Janine Billings of 480 East 94th Street."

Francesca Bernini-Winslow is my closest friend in the world. Her mother is an editor at one of the big fashion magazines, and rumor has it her father is a world-famous movie director, an Englishman. Her name is her mother's and the Winslow comes from her mother's grandfather, a modern painter and someone my grandmother dismisses as "decadent." He may have been a major flirt, but he's a good-enough artist to rate one entire corner in a room at the Museum of Modern Art.

Anyway, Francesca is a drama queen. She has been on the brink of the edge of Disaster since we were in pre-K together. She's gorgeous. I mean that quite literally. She has huge dark-blue eyes, awesome cheekbones, a nose she complains about constantly that sort of tilts and gives her face its uniqueness. She changes her hair color every other week. She's tall and thin, and clothes look great on her. She hasn't worn anything normal to class in years, but somehow she gets away with it. She has an aura about her. She's always had it. She knows and seems always to have known *everything*.

I'm saving up to go to Europe with Francesca for a year or two, instead of going to college. I don't mention this at home, of course. It would blow my parents away. The no-college-right-away, finding-ourselves-in-Europe plan is basically hers. I, of course, must struggle and save and work all summer long to afford this adventure. Francesca gets hundreds a week in spending money and is perpetually broke. It drives me crazy when she borrows from me, which she does constantly. She never pays me back. Still, she's irresistibly glamorous, original, exciting, and so unpredictable, after all these millions of years we've been friends, I never know what she'll do next.

My parents can't stand her. Neither can Alex. Neither can Brian, come to think of it; her one fan in our household is Mark. And he adores her. It's completely mutual. They seem to share a language, communicate on a special level accessible only to the two of them. His accident affected her drastically. She haunted the hospital while he was there, brought him a present every single day, and still shows up once a week or so laden with gifts and absolutely the wildest stories imaginable. She's the best possible therapy for Mark— he's on a high for days after one of her visits—so naturally my parents, even Alex, have softened toward her since this totally unexpected side of her multiple personality surfaced.

Take the other night. My mother finally went out for dinner with my father. I mean, she had not set foot outside of the apartment since Mark came home from the hospital. She trained her replacement at work with a million telephone calls and a mountain of faxes, but her guilt over not being right on the scene when Mark was hurt is ridiculous. (She was on location setting up for a fundraiser and ended up being the last to know about Mark.) She won't even let the cab driver share the blame.

Anyway, I was stuck sitting for Mark so she could have dinner with Daddy and some of his customers, and I didn't really mind or anything except I'd had to cancel other plans. I decided to invite Francesca over to lighten things up. She said she'd be right there and finally appeared two and a half hours later when Mark was nodding off and I had given up on her completely. She breezed in with her spiked hair and her crazy-quilt clothes, a flush in her cheeks that could have been from fresh air or a slight buzz, but Mark was so absolutely thrilled to see her, it made the long wait almost worth it.

"I brought you a book," she said, and when he looked disappointed she whipped it behind her back, out of his sight. Mark is small for his age and wears thick glasses, so he looked like a little old man propped against four or five pillows with the TV remote near his right hand the only thing that seemed to interest him in the slightest. "What's this?" Francesca confronted him. "Do I detect something less than boundless joy and gratitude? Is this the Mark I dream of, the man who makes all other men look dorky? Can he be—a *glom*?"

"A what?"

"A glom," she insisted, as though he should certainly know what that was. "A glib, obtuse mediocrity who never reads or thinks or wonders about anything."

"That sounds like me, all right." He sank gloomily against his pillows. He'd been in despair since Mom had left. He was convinced she had gone back to work, which didn't make much sense at this hour, but that possibility seemed to threaten him. He'd become tremendously possessive since she'd been hovering so relentlessly, at home and at the hospital.

Francesca threw her head back and shrilled with laughter. If this sounds a tad over the top, you had to be there, but it certainly got Mark's attention. And mine.

She held the book up like a trophy. It was one of the Dune series. Mark squinted at it through his thick glasses.

"I've read *The Chronicles of Narnia*," he said, plummeting back into the dumps.

"This isn't *Narnia*," she countered, thrusting it at him. "This is *Dune!*" And she slid to the floor just below him, weighed down in her overcoat, and began to read aloud. She was still reading more than an hour later when Mom and Dad came in. She flashed them a smile, turned the book over to Mark opened to the page she'd been reading, and left him utterly hooked and helpless to do anything but read on. She sailed out in one fluid motion, wishing everyone good night, accepting the gush of thanks from my parents and me, and assuring us she'd climb right into a taxi and call the minute she arrived at her apartment. She never called, of course, and it got too late to phone there, so I had to call Mom the instant I got to school the next morning to say she was alive and well and so sorry she'd forgotten to let us know.

"Did I say I'd call?" was what she really said. "I thought I told you I was meeting Gordon at Bouncer's."

It was Francesca who clued me in to Alan Gelber's true identity and solved the riddle of why he suddenly entered our lives, as they say on the soaps. She's amazing about a lot of things, but she's an absolute walking *Who's Who*.

"Alan Gelber is a researcher for *Weekend Closeup*," she said when I told her he'd been coming around a lot. He'd called and said Mom's ex-boss, Fischer Brocknaw, had suggested he call, and he came around that same day to the apartment.

Fischer Brocknaw has his own small consulting firm with a staff my mother describes as "enormously clever." She was working for Fischer when she met my father, and he gave them Baccarat crystal for their wedding and waited sixteen years to get her back. His story, not mine, but I get a kick out of him. Fischer and his staff advise the super-rich and powerful on everything from how to run a family wedding to raising money for a favorite charity to running for public office. My mother took care of the practical side, the "boring details" as she called them, but she must have done it awesomely, because Fischer phones about forty-three times a day trying to get her back again.

Anyway, Alan Gelber arrived and mostly wandered around after Mom, though she didn't seem too clear as to what he was doing there. He'd say things like "Don't let me interrupt," and he kept looking around as though he expected things to change or something.

He looks like an older version of this computer nerd in Alex's class, only Jason is better-looking. Alan Gelber has brown hair, a sallow complexion, and small features. His eyes are so small they'd probably disappear if he took his glasses off, and his clothes don't fit properly. It isn't because he's weirdly shaped or anything. They just don't fit. He has a quick, quiet way of speaking. If you're not listening, you won't even know he's talking. I cannot imagine Fischer Brocknaw putting up with him for more than four seconds, much less knowing him for "years" (as Gelber claims). Maybe he's his tax accountant or something.

"Why would *Weekend Closeup* be interested in us?" I asked Francesca.

She shrugged. "Your mother was a big, high-profile success. Maybe her boss is trying to zap her for leaving him."

"Does he do exposés?" I couldn't imagine what he could expose about our family that would bring on anything but yawns, but it rankled.

Francesca leveled me with one of her steady-on, full-wattage-from-those-dark-blue-eyes looks before she said, "Do you ever watch *Weekend Closeup*?"

"Sometimes. Not really. My father does. It comes on after his football."

"They totally ruined Roxanne's career."

I hadn't heard of Roxanne in months, I realized, and she'd had two platinum singles in less than six months, a year or so ago.

"Her whole image was that wild-girl bit," Francesca said. "*Weekend Closeup* found the boy she left behind—but not all that far behind—and blew her whole routine. He's a *pediatrician*, are you ready for that, and they're *married*! They've been secretly married for years."

I couldn't believe it. I'd had to hide Roxanne's albums when I bought them, the covers were so lurid. My parents despised her, and they were pretty cool about most things.

I went home and told my mother about Alan Gelber.

She smiled. "Francesca is something else. Fischer may be trying to zap me, but it's backfiring. I'm boring Mr. Gelber senseless. He's coming next week to 'wrap things up,' and I'm sure after that we'll be just another story filed in the dead drawer."

"*He* should be filed in the dead drawer," I sulked.

"He's all right. He cannot believe how straight we are."

"Did he say that?"

"Of course not. But it's obvious. He's an only child, and all the din around here drives him crazy. I think he'd find it acceptable if we were kooky, far-out, interesting. But it baffles him to realize how ordinary we are."

"How do you know he's an only child?"

"I asked him. His father is a doctor. His mother manages his father's office. Alan is the serious, bright product of two serious, bright parents, and the irony is he makes his living working in television. He basically hates television."

"Did he tell you that?"

"No, but it's obvious."

I wondered when things would begin to be obvious to me. "He does exposés."

"Yes." Mom looked mildly concerned about that.

"I think he's a creep."

"He may be. Fortunately there's nothing for him to be creepy about around here."

30.

"No adulterous love affairs, no cheating on SATs . . ."

"Cristina!" She was laughing, but I realized this jerk was making her nervous.

Gordon Larrimer is Francesca's latest boyfriend. She says he's hot, but he seems to me to be the coldest person on earth. He's very handsome, of course. Francesca only picks the gorgeous ones. Her discards stack up like some Best-Looking Men in America list. And Gordon may be the best-looking of the Best-Looking. He looks like something out of a Tommy Hilfiger ad. But he has no visible personality. He sort of stands around waiting for everyone to notice him, and everyone usually does. I've never heard him complete a sentence, and what he does say he mumbles, so you have to keep asking him what he said. He's totally noncommittal about everything, and he has a queer, blank, empty look in those big brown eyes.

"There's such a thing as being too handsome," my mother said, the one time she met him.

I'm not sure I follow that completely, but I agree with it anyway. And what makes me really crazy is how *wild* Francesca is over this guy. I mean, she always gets all steamed up when she's first dating someone, but they've been seeing each other for over a year now, and she's still gaga.

"He's slime" was my brother Alex's only comment, ages ago. It's like the worst thing Alex has ever said about anyone.

What bothers me most is how she acts when she's with him. I've already mentioned how changeable, unpredictable, schizoid she can be. When she's with Gordon—or when she's spent a lot of time with Gordon—she acts tentative, almost scared. She denies this, of course. I only had the guts

31.

to confront her with it once, and she got so testy denying it, we didn't speak for three weeks. I always cave in before she does.

My mother was suddenly there in the den with me. "Aren't you going to have some breakfast? Why are you dawdling around in here?"

I put down the newspaper, quashing the urge to hide it behind my back or ball it up so no one else could read about Janine Billings.

"Are you all right, Cristina?"

"I'm fine, Mom. A little tired. Groggy. You know me. I'm never too snappy first thing."

"Then go and get something to eat!" She smiled and gave me her How Many Times Do I Have To Say This? look.

"Okay, okay." I glanced back at the paper. I'd left it open to the back page. Folding it properly would make her wonder what I'd been reading, and that was the last thing I wanted. "I'm going to visit Brian later." I was moving out of the room, wondering if the grounding my father had threatened would become a reality. "He's probably feeling pretty sore."

"Fine," my mother agreed. "I can't seem to take in all that happened last night. We have to be grateful no one was seriously hurt."

Seriously. Try murdered. It's not possible. Murder is a kind of plot used for movies, novels, miniseries. Murder is a crime committed constantly in New York, but not to anyone *I* know.

Or don't know. Didn't know.

Like Janine Billings.

I wondered, as I slouched toward the kitchen and smells like bacon, fresh-brewed coffee, and something loaded with cinnamon, what it must be like to live like Francesca. And Markie. They had servants who cooked and cleaned and did their laundry and took their phone messages. Basically they lived on their own. No one to answer to, no one to keep track of them.

Alex and my father were arguing when I finally sat down to breakfast.

"Serve yourself," my mother said, gesturing toward the oven where she was keeping everything warm. "I'm taking Mark a tray. He seems to have developed a little cough."

I served myself, Mom left with Mark's tray, and Alex and my father were sulking when I sat back down. "I thought you had a pickup game," I said to my brother.

"Nobody else showed. Nice party you went to." He was cranky from his go-around with Dad. "How's Brian?"

"Okay."

"I've got something you should read," my father pursued Alex.

"Okay, Dad, okay." Alex hated fighting with anybody, but especially with Dad.

"I know what I'm talking about."

"I realize that, Dad."

"And I'm not preaching. I was *there*."

"Okay."

"When you've read what I'm going to give you, show it to that bleeding-heart liberal teacher of yours. He doesn't know what he's talking about."

Suddenly *I* knew what they were talking about.

My father was born in Cuba. People don't know he's from anywhere other than New York City unless he tells them (mostly he doesn't). He was born in Havana and raised in a small residence hotel there, the Olympic, which his parents managed, until he was sent to prep school in the States at the tender age of eleven. From then until he graduated (summa cum laude) from college, he went back to Cuba only for summers, though he'd always planned finally to live there. He did too, until Fidel arrived. Enter Fidel, exit Dad. I suppose Mom and Mark and Alex and I should be grateful to *El Jefe*, 'cause if Dad had stayed there, we wouldn't be here, but we don't even own a Castro convertible, and they're not related.

The really interesting thing though is that Dad was brought up in this little hotel. To hear Mamita, my Cuban grandmother, tell it, my father was a sort of male version of Eloise at the Plaza: bright, lively, curious; and he began to play serious bridge at the age of five.

"Sometimes," Mamita likes to tell it—"we would be missing a fourth for our game, and Eduardo"—my father—"would be standing there. He loved to watch us play. Finally Mrs. Sussmann, I think it was, asked him to join the game. From the beginning he was wonderful: serious, attentive, quick. And he loved it. Even Dr. Bremer came to enjoy him, and he had objected strongly in the beginning. 'This is not a child's game,' he would say, but Eduardo did not play as a child, never."

My father still plays tournament bridge. In fact, his old friend Harry Langer told me bridge was the first clue anybody had to Daddy's romance with Mom: He missed his regular Wednesday-night game with Harry and the boys, a game that at that time was four years old and is still going strong. It was the only time he missed it for what I know they considered a silly reason. If my father is in New York on a Wednesday evening, he plays bridge with his regular foursome.

He and my mother met at a cocktail party, one of those mob scenes where everybody stands around in little groups looking at everyone else. Mom swept in with Fischer (he's still the most glamorous escort in New York) and floated around until she was introduced to Daddy, whose last name (Garcia-Vasquez) she mistook for that of a very controversial Colombian novelist. Since she had just read this guy's book, she starts showing off, throwing all these questions at Daddy about the book, and Daddy, who hadn't read it but caught on to her gaffe right away, played along and gave her a really hard time, acting offended and annoyed to the point where she began to worry that she'd actually hurt him. By the time she found out she'd been had, she was too attracted or something to be deeply and importantly (or permanently) angry. He went bonkers too, apparently, because within six days they were engaged, and my maternal grandmother still complains about how little time she had to pull together The Wedding. The pictures in the album are great, but the only one who remembers every detail about the day is my mother's mother. Mamita was still in Cuba and not allowed to come to share in her only child's biggest moment.

What I'm trying to say is that to look at us, you'd think we were your average upper-middle-class upper east side New York family (if there is such a thing), but we've got our "exotic" side. My college counselor at school shrieked with laughter when Daddy suggested including the fact that he's Hispanic on my college admissions form. "Mr. Garcia-Vasquez," she tittered, lisping "Vasque*th*" in her best Castilian, her control and rock-solid refinement obviously threatened by what had caught her—hilariously—by surprise, "you are *hardly* Hispanic!" I have never seen her so unhinged, before or since. Her name is Emma Walpole, she has white hair rinsed blue and coiffed within an inch of its life, and she could not reconcile Hispanic with my father's prep-school and Ivy League college credentials. I really dig that side of my heritage. The Irish-English side is so *repressed*.

Anyway, now you know where I'm coming from (entirely). My mother's decision to go back to work had more to do with the outrageous tuitions at our three private schools than anything else. My father put himself on a real guilt trip about it at first, and that was compounded by his mother-in-law's instant disapproval. My grandmother lives in an apartment in the same building as ours, two floors up. In fact, our apartment used to belong to her; my mother grew up in it. But when my grandfather died and my parents were looking for someplace big enough for all of us, my grandmother sold them our apartment and moved upstairs. She's really cool, but she never ever approved of my mother having a career.

Mom did so well from her first day back on the job, it was hard to feel guilty or annoyed or even abandoned (my reaction) for very long. My grandmother outlasted us all, of course, but I've overheard her bragging about Mom's success to her bridge friends on more than one occasion.

Now, suddenly, with the shock of Mark's accident, Mom is home; constantly, immovably here.

"Cristina!" It was my father, and I had a sense he'd been trying to bring me out of my little trance for some time.

"Sorry, Daddy."

"Who's this Alan Gelber fellow? Have you met him?"

"Sure. He's a researcher for *Weekend Closeup*. He's a major nerd."

"I thought your mother told me he wasn't interested in us."

"That's what she told me."

"Well, he's on the phone with her. Right now."

"I don't have a clue, Daddy." What if Gelber had found out Janine Billings and I had been at the same party? Down, girl. That's not possible.

"I answered the phone, just now, and he started asking me a lot of questions," my father said.

"About what?" *Oh, God . . .*

"Cuba. For Pete's sake. I left there over forty years ago. The Cuba I knew doesn't exist anymore."

I watched him warm his hands around his coffee mug, his thoughts taking him a lot farther away than I had just been. I had a bad case of the jitters, so I went to see Mark. He was coughing his head off. Mom is always bugging him to keep moving around. "You'll get congested," she warns him constantly. Mark is a TV addict; he'd rather watch TV than breathe. So now he wasn't breathing so easily.

He hadn't eaten much from the bed tray arched over his knees, and if there's anything more revolting to look at than cold eggs, I don't know what it is. They sort of *wither* on the plate.

"Can you fix the picture?" he rasped, pointing to the little TV set Dad had rented for his convalescence. Mom disapproved of this from day one. It always seemed to be on when he was awake. "He won't want to get out of bed," Mom railed at Dad. "He has to keep moving, be as mobile as possible."

"He has a cast on his leg," Dad tried to soften her. "He'll move."

"Not if he has a TV in his bedroom."

I fiddled with the dials, and a picture reemerged from the spinning, diagonally striped blur of color. He was watching *Gilligan's Island.*

"Mark! These are the world's oldest reruns."

"I like them. I know all the words."

I picked up his tray. "Do you want something else?"

He shook his head. That started him coughing again.

"Where'd you get a cold from? I bet Laney Conlon kissed you when she came to see you yesterday."

Laney Conlon lives in our building, is in the fourth grade at my school, and has been in love with Mark since she was in a stroller.

He got a little flushed and glared at me, and when people wear glasses as thick as Mark's, glares are intense. "That's

38.

all she's good for," he wheezed. "Germs." Then he thought about it. "She didn't come near me!"

"Do you want to play cards or something? I'm going to take your tray to the kitchen, but I can come back."

He shook his head against his mound of pillows and was racked with coughing. I couldn't handle it. I took the tray to the kitchen and then went looking for Mom. She was in the den with Dad, going over bills.

"Is Mark okay?" She never misses.

"He's coughing a lot."

"It's looser, though. He doesn't have a temperature anymore. Check the water level in his humidifier, will you? I think it's helping."

"Maybe we should call Dr. Meyerson." Dad. He freaked when we tracked him down after the accident. He was in Venezuela. He canceled the rest of his business trip, almost two weeks' worth of super-crucial appointments, and flew right home. Then he and Mom camped in the hospital until Mark was discharged.

Mark was hit by the cab at four-fifteen on a Wednesday afternoon. The cab did run a red light, but Mark never looks where he's going. He was crossing Lexington Avenue, coming from the candy store where he always goes right after school to buy a treat and play video games. The storekeeper recognized him but didn't know his last name or his address. The manager of the pharmacy next door did, and I got the first call. I was the only one home. I'll never forget it. I was writing a report on *Madame Bovary*.

"Is this Mrs. Garcia-Vasquez?" a man asked me. *"¿Habla inglés, señora?"*

"I am not Mrs. Garcia-Vasquez," I said, and I'm sure I was

sort of rude. We get calls from all kinds of Hispanic groups and publications, and I wasn't in the mood to deal with it. I was basically stuck on *Madame Bovary*, and I wanted to go out that night to the movies or anywhere. If this paper wasn't done, there was no way unless I fudged about having it finished.

"Is Mrs. Garcia-Vasquez at home? This is Patrolman Perez of the Nineteenth Precinct."

Our local precinct. "My mother is at work. She can't be reached right now."

"How about your father? Do you have his number at work?"

"He's away on business. In Venezuela."

"Is there anyone—?"

"What's the matter?"

"Is there anyone else there with you?"

"My grandmother lives upstairs."

A pause. "How old is your grandmother?"

"Eighty-three. What's—?"

"May I have her name and number, please?"

Now it was my turn to hesitate. "How do I know—?"

"How old are you?"

"Sixteen."

"Are you alone there?"

I didn't answer.

"Miss Garcia-Vasquez, I'm sorry to be asking all these questions, but there's been an accident."

"Where? Who?"

"Just tell me your grandmother's name, please."

"How do I know who you are?"

"You can check it out, miss. You can call the precinct— 555-6371—and ask to speak to Patrolman Perez. Ignacio Perez. Badge number 6548990. Did you get all that?"

"Wait!" I was writing frantically.

He repeated all the numbers and his name. "Call right away," he told me. "It's very urgent." And he hung up.

Alex got home then and I told him everything I knew in a semicoherent rush. He called the precinct and was put right through to Patrolman Perez, who proceeded to tell him about Mark. By that time Mark had been rushed to the hospital. We didn't have cab fare between us, so we dashed upstairs to borrow it from Gram, only she wouldn't lend it to us until we told her what was going on, and then she insisted on coming too.

We kept calling home from the hospital. We talked to several doctors who were working on Mark, but we hadn't been allowed to see him. Gram knew one of the doctors, and she signed the permission for them to operate. There seemed to be an incredible urgency about everything.

I was staring at the big clock in the hospital waiting room when Mom finally answered the phone at the apartment. It was nine forty-five. I could not remember her ever arriving home later.

"Alan Gelber's coming here tomorrow," my mother told me now. "He's talking as though they're really going to tape a segment on us in the next few weeks. Here." She glanced around the den. "I won't let them in this room, of course. The living room's not too bad. I've been meaning to have it painted."

"Why should they want to tape us?" I asked.

41.

My father didn't look up from his crossword puzzle. "We really have no idea."

Let's hope Gelber has no idea, I prayed, heading for the shower.

Brian was watching the football game when I arrived. He looked rosy cheeked and wonderful. He glanced around to be sure his parents weren't in sight, and then he pulled me over and kissed me. He tasted salty, like potato chips, which he'd been devouring.

"How're you doing?" I asked him.

"I'm pretty sore." He shifted the bandaged arm slightly. "Sorry my mom called yours."

"That's okay. My dad freaked. They're both calming down. But they don't know about anything but you."

He made a face. "What else is there to know?"

"That girl who was screaming during the fight—her name was Janine Billings."

"Was?"

"She's dead, Bri. Murdered." I whispered this.

"Say *what*?"

I nodded my head. I simply could not repeat what I had just told him.

We both jumped when Brian's mother appeared. "There's a call for you, Cristina." She gestured toward the extension on a nearby table.

It was Markie. "Somebody stole stuff from here yesterday!" she blurted. "A lot of stuff: money, jewelry—"

"What are you talking about? Somebody at the party?"

"*Yes!* My dad always leaves a lot of cash for me when he goes away—a lot of cash—and when I found that was missing, I checked out some of the hiding places where my mother keeps her jewelry. That's gone too. Everything's *gone!*" She started to cry. I couldn't remember Markie crying ever before. She's a tomboy and a tough lady, and crying is strictly for babies in her book. (And mine.)

"Hold on. Do you want me to come over and help you look?"

Brian's team scored a touchdown and he went wild. No chance he was eavesdropping on this conversation. He might have forgotten I was even there.

"I've torn this place apart," she sobbed. "It's gone!"

"Okay. Don't panic. I'll be right there."

"Maybe it was that scum Gordon brought."

"Who?" I knew who. What I hadn't known was that Gordon Larrimer brought him. Did Francesca know it?

"Nicky—Ricky—some name like that."

"Nicky Baylor." I filled it in. "He came with Janine Billings." *Now* Brian was staring at me.

"Right," Markie remembered. "Nicky Baylor. Scum."

"You haven't heard, then."

"Heard what?"

"I'll tell you when I get there."

"Why are you going over there?" Brian wanted to know. "You have to tell me about—you know."

I spotted the first section of the Sunday *Times* nearby. I

opened it to the inside back page and handed it to him. "It's all here." I sat there while he read it.

"Whoa!" When he looked up at me, his eyes were huge.

"Can you believe it? I cannot *believe* it."

He started reading it again.

I stood up. I really didn't want to go to Markie's. "I'll come back later, Brian."

There was no sign of the battle waged in Markie's living room, and her doorman was a lot friendlier. Markie, however, was a basket case. She kept darting around like someone crazed. She showed me the drawer where the cash had been kept. It had a false back, and the drawer had to be pulled out completely to remove this false back, like a card from an index file. The area behind it was absolutely empty.

"I've never shown anyone this before," she sniffed, trying hard not to cry anymore. Her face was puffy from it. She led me into her mother's room—her parents have separate bedrooms with an adjoining bathroom—and we walked into her mother's closet, which is the neatest, most elegant closet I've ever seen. It has mirrors and shelves for shoes and handbags and rows and rows of dresses, suits, slacks, coats. Behind one full-length mirror is a door leading to a tiny space and a small nest of drawers, which Markie pulled out now to reveal odds and ends: hair clips, gloves, sunglasses, and bits of what looked to me like costume jewelry.

"She keeps the really good stuff in the bank," Markie said. "But certain pieces she wears a lot, she keeps in here."

"Maybe she took them with her. She probably—"

"I know what she took with her, Cris! She says good

jewelry is tacky in California, so she takes a lot of junk. She told me she was leaving this stuff here just before she went away. She'd planned to put it in the bank with everything else, but she ran out of time."

"Are you sure it was here yesterday?"

Markie nodded. "I check on it every day. I'm like that. My mother doesn't ask me to do much for her, so—" She burst into tears. "My grandmother's diamond ring was in there!"

We went into her bedroom. Unless there's a party, visiting Markie means spending every minute in her bedroom. She's got everything in there: TV, VCR, CD player, stereo, even a small upright piano. It's a very large, comfortable room, but it struck me how weird it is to have such an enormous apartment and only live in one of its rooms.

She sprawled all over her king-size bed. "I don't know what to do, Cris."

She didn't have to explain. When her parents found out about the missing items, they'd know she'd had a party. Didn't they expect her to have parties once in a while? They were gone all the time.

"I called Francesca. She's coming over."

I stared at her. "Did she tell you anything?"

"About what?"

"Markie, that friend of Gordon's—Nicky Baylor. He brought a girl to your party."

"Janine Billings. I know. She's as slimy as he is."

"She's dead, Markie. She was murdered last night." Then I told her what I knew. I felt like a radio newscaster delivering a breaking story for the fifth time. The terrible fact of what I was repeating was beginning to seem less real.

Frieda, the Hannigans' housekeeper forever and ever,

stuck her head in. "Dinner's in the freezer, Markie. Hello, Miss Cristina. It's my seafood casserole, the one you love. It's marked with today's date and the microwave instructions. I'm off to my sister's. I'll be back before ten."

"What did Frieda say about the theft?" I asked when she'd gone.

"I didn't tell her. It was her night off."

I couldn't believe it. Markie usually tells Frieda everything. Frieda is the closest thing to a parent Markie has. "Why not?"

Markie started to cry again. "She always warns me about having parties. And she freaks out about anything that gets lost or broken. One time a cufflink of my father's was missing, and Frieda got all bent out of shape and kept saying, 'They blame me. They blame me.' I was pretty little, but I'll never forget how frantic she got."

"Your parents would never blame—"

Markie shuddered away a sob. "Who knows who they'd blame? It's not Frieda's problem, anyway. It's mine."

Francesca arrived. "Have you told her?" she asked me right away.

"Maybe whoever killed Janine stole all the stuff that was taken from here," Markie said. "Maybe Nicky Baylor—"

I couldn't stand this. "Someone's been *killed*!"

"I hardly knew her," Markie whined. "And her date came in here, broke up the place, caused a big fight, slashed Brian, and stole stuff."

"You don't know that he stole anything," I put in.

"Who else? George Benson? He couldn't walk. Jeff Lawlor? Pete McKay? Andy Villard?"

"You know all those guys," I said. "There were lots of people here you didn't know."

"Girls can steal as well," Francesca said. "Janine would do anything for Nicky."

"Your sympathy is overwhelming," I said.

"How about Gordon?" Markie sneered. "Gordon brought that scum."

Francesca rolled her eyes. "I was absolutely appalled when Gordon showed up with them yesterday." She was shifting, as I had seen her do so often, shedding her feistiness for a softer, friendlier role. She is utterly impossible to predict. "Nicky is such a loser. Gordon allows people like that to hang off him periodically. I don't know whether they feed his insatiable ego or if he has a well-hidden compassionate side. In any case, they're never around for long. One thing Gordon doesn't have is a high tolerance level."

Markie looked confused.

Francesca shook her head. "I just can't shake that image."

"What image?" I watched Markie move ahead of us down the long hallway. She was obsessing about the missing items.

"That nightmare footage of Janine's body on the subway platform. Of course the body is covered, you can't really see anything, but knowing it's Janine . . ."

I shuddered.

We searched every inch of that enormous apartment. I'd never been in some of those rooms. They were all beautiful, perfectly appointed, pristine, but they had absolutely no character, like rooms in a posh hotel.

We found nothing.

"I'm going back to Brian's." We were heading back to Markie's room to hang out. "My mother might call there looking for me."

"I left this number on my answering machine," Francesca said. She had no one to go home to. Her mother was in Europe. I knew that when she invited me over earlier. I was never invited when her mother was home; nobody was.

"They'll never connect Janine to my party, will they?" Markie worried as she walked me to the elevator.

"Why would they?"

"That's all I need." She bit her lip. She seemed to be all cried out.

Brian was in his room taking a nap by the time I got back there. "He doesn't want to admit it," his mother told me, "but this has taken a lot out of him."

I had nowhere to go but home. I ran into my grandmother on the elevator. She's really cool, and she dresses really well and looks a lot younger than she is. We hugged, and then we got to my floor.

"I'm rushing, as usual," she said, stepping off with me. "My bridge game ran longer than expected, and I'm supposed to go out for dinner in less than an hour. How's everything with you?"

I was desperate to tell her. Everything. Sometimes, not a lot, but sometimes when Mom's overreacting to every breath I take, I go to see Gram. I can tell her anything, and she always listens, waits for me to finish, and then talks to me. She's much more laid back than my mother. She says the only reason to be a parent is to be a grandparent.

She was obviously rushing, though I knew if I wanted to talk, she'd make time for me.

I pushed the button for the elevator and it was still there; the doors opened immediately. "Everything's cool, Gram," I lied. If she hadn't been rushing, she'd probably have given me one of her piercing Looks, but she *was* rushing. I waved good-bye as the elevator doors slid shut. I think the only meal my grandmother eats at home is breakfast. She has a social life that won't quit.

Everybody was in the den watching *Weekend Closeup*. I kept on to my room. I was craving a cigarette. Alex suddenly appeared, headed for his room. Since he's death on my smoking, I slid the cigarette back into its pack.

"How's Brian?" he asked me.

"Okay. He's sleeping at the moment."

"Nice people you hang out with."

"I didn't even know the boy! Nobody did."

"Who let him in? What was he doing there? You guys are totally out of control."

I was sick of the whole subject. "Is the program over?"

"No, but I have better things to do. It's pretty dull, anyway."

"Why are they watching it?"

"That guy is coming tomorrow. Gelber. They want to do a segment on us."

"Why?"

Alex shook his head. "Don't ask me. The only thing duller than what I just watched is us." He retreated into his room before I could say anything.

Alex has applied for early action at Yale. That means he could know before Christmas where he'll be going to college. We could all use that kind of super good news right now, but Alex doesn't think he'll be accepted. Even though our dad went to Yale. Even though Alex is an A–/B+ student, varsity everything from sophomore year on, and editor of his school newspaper. His college counselor told him there's nothing "different" about him, and coming from an upper-middle-class Manhattan family with all the advantages is a major drawback at the hottest college in the northeastern pack. It doesn't make a lot of sense to me, but Alex said he was sorely tempted to create a new ID for himself on the application, like saying he was adopted by our parents when he was nine, and before that he'd lived in a string of foster homes, rejected out of every one.

"I could say I don't know who my real parents are, but I'll never rest till I find them. Something like that."

"Why would you—?"

He shrugged. "Get their attention. The oddballs have the best shot in this league."

I feel for him, I really do. It's times like these that make me glad I've decided to put going to college on hold. Eleventh grade in my school can be described in one word: nightmare. Try *Pressure* with a capital *P*. Everyone carries a full load academically, going for honors wherever possible, plus Achievements and as many bouts with SATs as it takes to break twelve hundred. Plus choosing colleges, deciding whether to apply early, then trying to salvage some self-esteem when the school counselor tells you what your chances really are and where.

I have two very close friends who took their junior years

in Europe just to escape the snakepit back home. That sounds like a cool move, party time in the Old World and all that, but we are talking high school here, and it's not all that easy to pack up and go abroad on your own at the ripe old age of sixteen.

Anyway, when I complained bitterly to Francesca about all of this, she rolled her eyes.

"What's your solution?" I snapped, wondering why she hadn't gone abroad and knowing it was because this whole college scene didn't panic her at all. She never got upset when I did or over the same things.

"Forget college," she said, as though it was so obvious. "What do you need college for? Think about it. You are a computer whiz. You have been since fifth grade. You've had good jobs for the past couple of summers because of it. That means you are employable. You could move in with someone—well, you have a bit of growing up to do in that department. You could come to Europe with me and *find* yourself."

As often happens when Francesca is lecturing, I couldn't think of a thing to say.

"Look at it this way," she went on. "We've been in this overpriced brain factory for twelve excruciating years. We've been taking college-level courses for the past three. If I hear one more time what a cinch freshman year will be— at any of these pricey citadels—I shall scream for as long as my voice holds out. Everyone I know who's 'gone on' to college from here does one of two things: dies of boredom and drops out before Christmas, or gets onto a superfast track academically and shoots so far ahead of the peer group, misfit and misery go hand-in-hand with utter drudgery. There is a third group who lose all control with their first taste of freedom away from home and party right out the door, but they are not our sort. They usually come from tiny little towns and have to take precalculus in summer school to catch up to the rest of us."

"I have to go to college," was all I could think of to say.

"Why? Your brother will go to college. He wants to go. He should go. He will do beautifully. That should be enough for your parents."

"It won't be."

She smiled and shook her head slowly. "Then I can't help you. Take your place. Stand in the appointed slot. Stay in your narrow, deepening little groove. But I know you best, Cristina. I know you have dreams to fly on. The really heavy stuff makes you giggle, just the way it makes me giggle. You're not meant to tag along, prissy Crissy. Not my friend who thought of using clear plastic wrap to cover the toilet seats in the faculty john."

"Francesca!" That was in ninth grade. No one had ever found out who'd done it.

"*I'll* never tell, you *know* that. I just hate to see all that talent—homogenized."

It was easy, after that. I just don't think about it. And when I have to think about it, I pretend it's all solved. I'm not going to college. That's that.

I am chronically late to school. I don't mean to be late; I'm not late on purpose. I can't seem to get this across to Mrs. Walpole. I was fine when my mother was walking me to school every day, grades pre-K through seven. I wish Mrs. Walpole would take that into account when she doles out all this penalty time for lateness. I mean, if time were bankable, I'd have had millions in available funds when I began to lapse into my current and really boring string of late arrivals. I do not stall around at home watching the clock to be sure I'm already late before I dash out the front door. Things *happen*, every day. Elevators take forever to arrive, I miss every crossing traffic light, people ask me directions and I can't just rush by them. That's rude. Things happen.

I was twenty minutes late to school the Monday after Markie's party, and when I saw this crowd of people outside the front door and realized they were reporters (holding pads or microphones) and photographers (carrying—and using—elaborate camera equipment), I didn't think too much about it. We have some celebrity kids in our school, so we've had media attention before. Race Rancor's daughter Ruby is in ninth grade, Senator Standish's granddaughter is in fourth, and a girl in my class, Adelaide Courter, dates a famous hockey player. His limo, license plate PUCK, picks her up every afternoon right at school. I can never remember his name, but Alex knows who he is and is wildly impressed with Adelaide, though he never admits it, of course.

"He's one of the greats," Alex complains when I can't remember the hockey player's name.

"Fine," I come back. "All I know is he's a lot shorter than she is."

The Monday after Markie's party, though, the media crowd made a move on *me*, flashbulbs popping, microphones pointing like a lot of accusing index fingers. I waved them off.

"I'm nobody," I said to one. Somebody else got in my face. "I'm really late."

They all shouted at once: "Were you at the party?" "Did you know Janine Billings well?" "How long have you known Markie Hannigan?"

I kept moving straight ahead, but my heart had begun to pound, and it took all my strength to open the front door to my school. My next shock was finding Mrs. Walpole in the vestibule. She pulled me inside and locked the door behind me.

"You are impossible, Cristina! This has been the worst morning of my life, and your being late has compounded it."

"I'm really sorry, Mrs. Walpole. What's going on?"

She leveled me with a Don't Even Think About Conning Me look. "Did you go to Markie's party?"

"Yes, ma'am."

"Well, that's what's going on. A girl who also went there was found murdered a short time later."

"I heard. But how—"

"She had Markie's address on a piece of paper in one of her pockets. You'll have to go upstairs to the junior lounge.

54.

The police are interviewing everyone who was at Markie's party."

My knees had turned to jelly, but I was still amazed when Mrs. Walpole guided me into the elevator. This is off-limits to students unless you have a cast on your leg or a doctor's note saying stair climbing will give you cardiac arrest. She pushed the button for the second floor, which is where the junior lounge is located.

Juniors and seniors at my school are permitted their own "lounges": old classrooms furnished with cast-off sofas and chairs that once graced the lobby or some faculty member's office and now qualify for the junk heap. But having one's own hangout is a great privilege, earned by actually making it to junior or senior year, and we are the envy of the rest of the school. Keeping each lounge looking like it has just been blitzed is a point of honor and involves considerable competition. Ours wins, hands down. The seniors cannot compare with our slovenly ways.

The presence of a teacher in either lounge is a rarity and means someone is in major trouble. The presence of an actual policeman (two, in fact) was utterly surreal, but I couldn't fully comprehend it since by now I was feeling importantly ill.

"This is the last." Mrs. Walpole introduced me as she held the door for me to enter the lounge. She followed me in. The Worst Morning of Her Life apparently included remaining in the Loathsome Lounge, as our room is lovingly called, for as long as this gathering might last.

The two uniformed policemen stood at the far end of the room, where a blackboard had once hung and where dubious rock-band posters and a free-form mural of questionable taste and subject matter done by our most talented class artist, Ellie Blair, now formed a really bizarre sort of tapestry behind them. One was heavyset, with a bulge above his gun belt. The other was taller, thinner, with a face like a ferret. He would have made a perfect Javert in *Les Misérables*.

That thought made me sicker. I slumped onto the nearest sofa, realizing after I sank almost to the floor (this particular sofa had nothing left, supportwise), I was sitting right next to Francesca. She gave me her best Can You Believe This? look and then quickly glanced away.

"Could you give us your name, please?" the heavyset policeman asked me.

"Cristina Garcia-Vasquez," Leslie Quinn said. Leslie answers every question asked in class too, whether she's the one being asked or not. She's supersmart and pretty obnoxious about it.

"Please let the young lady answer for herself," Ferret-Face told Leslie.

"Cristina Garcia-Vasquez," I repeated. I had to clear my throat before I could muster any voice at all.

"Were you at Markie Hannigan's party on Saturday?"

"Yes, sir."

"Did you see Janine Billings there?"

"Yes, sir. I didn't know her very well. I just knew her name. We'd never had a conversation or anything."

"You weren't a friend of hers?"

"No, sir."

"I find it very strange that no one here was friendly with Miss Billings prior to Saturday night. Yet she was present at a very fancy private party." The heavyset policeman looked around at each of us before he went on. "Please tell us what happened at the party, Miss Garcia-Vasquez. Did you witness the fight that took place?"

I told him what I remembered. I think I rambled on too much and went into too much detail. (I was incredibly nervous, but I tend to do that, nervous or not.) Both policemen looked utterly unaffected throughout, since this had to be the umpteenth telling of this tale and they had to be bored senseless.

"Thank you," the heavyset officer said when I was finished. "Has anyone anything to add at this time?"

No one moved.

"Okay," he concluded. "You've been very cooperative and we appreciate it. You've all signed the sheet we passed around with your name, address, and phone number."

I hadn't, but somebody handed it to me now and I did.

"One last piece of advice before we wrap this up," the officer went on. "There's been considerable media interest in this case. You never know what will appeal to the press, but the fact that this crime was committed among people of—privilege may seem like a welcome change from the endless casualty lists in the poorer neighborhoods. In any case, beware what you say to the press. They have a way of misinterpreting and misrepresenting, and what you tell them in all honesty and innocence may read quite differently. Our advice is to say 'No comment.' And don't overdo talking about this among yourselves. There's nothing to be accomplished by it, and you never know who might be listening."

I was tempted to go right back home after that, but the

thought of pushing my way past those reporters kept me in school. It may have been the longest day of my life until I realized I had Drama Club last period.

I guess most of what I've said about my school has been kind of bleak: drugs, alcohol, sex, and other sin at an early age. It's all there, of course, and I haven't even mentioned the anorexia and bulimia that plague the seventh, eighth, and ninth grades. Or Rachel Gann's abortion, which she had last year. Rachel's been on the Pill since she was thirteen, but she forgets to take it a lot, and she wasn't clear at all on who the father was. Her mother died when Rachel was really little and her father tries awfully hard. He comes to all the parent-teacher nights at school. But he's a very big deal physician, chief of staff in one of the best private hospitals, and Rachel, like Markie, Francesca, and a lot of other kids in my school, has been on her own for years.

On the other hand, I've been in Drama Club since fourth grade and would rather be in Drama Club than anywhere else in the world. It's mostly because of Mrs. Halladay—Karen Halladay, who plays Amanda, the lethal older woman who's always seducing the eligible young bucks on the television soap *Westport Diary*. She's nothing like Amanda, of course, and I have no idea why she's stayed on as our drama coach, but she's awesome. She directs two productions a year, one before Christmas and one in the spring, and I've had a speaking part in every one since sixth grade. Right now I have the lead in *The Merchant of Venice*. We do Shakespeare every other year. And we always have boys in the cast. We do open auditions with the boys' schools in the neighborhood—there must be eight within a twelve-block radius, if you include both sides of the park. Rob Emerson is Shylock, and he's really great. He and I were in *Ah, Wilderness!* in ninth grade and *The Boy Friend* last year. We do a musical every other year, the year we don't do Shakespeare.

Anyway, Drama Club is really something. It demands a lot of time and energy, and Mrs. Halladay is as tough as she can be. She runs rehearsal schedule like the army. Miss rehearsal once and you'd better have been in the hospital. Miss more than once and you're out. No matter who you are, no matter what your part. She organizes a strong backup system of understudies, and there's been a lot of grumbling that she encourages cutthroat competition and dirty tactics, but that's not true. She told us a long time ago how rough it is staying on the soap opera, dealing with the day-in, day-out grind, fighting to keep the character fresh and interesting.

"Go stale," she told us, "get lazy or complacent or cocky, and the next script you read, you'll find your character has a terminal disease or has disappeared."

Mrs. Halladay is not someone you get close to. But she's someone I depend on. She's fair, she treats everybody exactly alike, and if she tells you you're good, believe it. She almost never tells anyone that.

She has made Drama Club fun, challenging, exciting. We don't just learn lines; we learn all about how the play came to be written, about the playwright, about earlier productions and the actors who played our parts. I've learned more about the theater and certain aspects of the literature of the theater in Drama Club than in any academic courses offered in my school.

But more than that, doing the shows, being part of the

cast, finally standing out there in front of an audience (we run five performances per production, with two shows, including a matinee, on the final Saturday) is such an incredible high, such a transforming, inside-out thrill, I still don't know how I'm going to survive when I can no longer be part of it. My closest friends come from Drama Club associations. Francesca got me into Drama Club. She is the stage manager. Can you stand it? Her life is more dramatic than most of the plays we do, and she insists on being a techie.

Neva Williams is in Drama Club, its most talented member. Neva calls herself The Great Experiment because she is one of the first black girls ever to go to my school. She was brought into pre-K on a full scholarship. We have lots of black kids now, most of them just as well off as the rest of us and some of them celebrity kids, like Hally Stephenson. Her father is a big movie producer, but her mother is Lila Grey. *The* Lila Grey.

"Nice party Markie had," Neva murmured to me as Mrs. Halladay blocked a scene neither of us is in. Neva is playing Nerissa to my Portia. She's so good, she should always play the lead, but Mrs. Halladay is super fair about distributing parts.

"Where were you?" I asked her.

"I had to go somewhere with my mother and my little brother. I was ripping about missing it, but now I'm glad I did. That's all this saga needs—a black girl to blame it on!"

I giggled, and Mrs. Halladay stopped blocking to stare at me. She resumed what she had been doing immediately.

A couple of reporters were still hanging around when we left school.

"You were at the party, weren't you?" one of them asked me, chasing me to the corner.

I didn't react. Neva was with me. We usually walk together as far as her subway. She huddled into her denim jacket.

"Hey, girls, give us a break!" he begged. But when the light changed and we charged across the street, he didn't follow.

"I can't handle this," I muttered to Neva. "We didn't even know Janine Billings."

"Where'd you get that idea?" She gave me a very skeptical sideways glance.

"Nobody knew her," I assured her. "Well, I guess Gordon knew her slightly, since his friend dated her."

"Forget slightly," Neva said. "Ask your great friend Francesca about Janine Billings."

I stared at her. Neva and Francesca hate each other. My mother once theorized it was because Neva "upstaged" Francesca. I keep way out of it, since I really like both of them. "What do you mean?" I finally asked Neva, wondering if she'd tell me.

She laughed, knowing and not telling, a favorite ploy of hers. We reached the subway entrance and she plunged down the steps with a wave. "Later!"

Who *was* Janine Billings?

Alan Gelber was waiting in the lobby of my building when I got home from school.

"Your mother's out grocery shopping," Jerry, our doorman, told me grimly. My father once described Jerry as dour and, when I didn't know what that meant, made me look it up in the dictionary. It means gloomy, sullen, and that certainly sums up Jerry. He doesn't even cheer up at Christmas when he gets all that tip money from the tenants. "Your grandmother's with Mark," he went on now, "and I didn't think she'd appreciate someone unexpected arriving."

"I'm not due here for another hour," Gelber said. He wasn't apologizing or anything, just stating the fact of it.

I didn't know what to do, so I said, "Okay," to nobody in particular, and when Gelber followed me to the elevator, Jerry didn't stop him. We rode in silence for a couple of floors.

"You go to school around here," he finally said.

"Eight blocks away." Why would he care? He probably knew it anyway.

"Like it?"

I shrugged. "I've been there for twelve years."

"You smart or social?"

"Neither."

We had arrived, and I let myself and him in. "It's me, Gram!" I shouted, a family ritual.

Gelber was looking around as though he'd never been there before. What on earth was he looking for? I dropped my backpack with its four hundred pounds of books. I carry everything back and forth to school every day, I'm so paranoid I'll forget something.

"You look like your mother," he said. He was staring.

I tried not to squirm. "People say that. Actually, some people think I look like my father. In fact, a lot of people think my parents look alike, which is really scary considering . . ." *Bag it!*

"You going to college?"

"Doesn't everyone?"

"No. Not at all. Is there something you'd rather do?"

"Not really."

"Where are you thinking of applying?"

"I haven't gotten that far."

"With your options? You should have a long list. If you're seriously considering it at all, that is."

"We're into my brother's applications at the moment."

He nodded. "You're pretty close to your brother, right?"

"I guess so."

"Seems like he has it all: looks, brains, talent, drive." He made it sound excessive.

"Alex works hard."

Gelber smiled. It is not an expression he's comfortable with.

"Alex is amazing," I insisted.

"There's a remarkable lack of intrafamilial competitiveness here. I expect a certain amount of hero worship from the little guy, but you and your older brother really do get along."

"Bor-ring!" I blew it off.

"Why do you feel you have to trivialize it?"

I had had it. It was my turn to stare. "Don't you ever get sick of prying?"

"Why so defensive?"

"I'm not. I guess I just don't understand why you should be so interested."

"Do I threaten you? Does my being around make you nervous? You have a very interesting family."

"Really." That made it sound like I didn't agree, and I do agree, only I didn't think he was being straight with me, if that makes any sense at all.

"If I were you, I probably wouldn't go to college," he said. "Not right away, anyway."

My mouth may have dropped open. I hope not.

He cracked up. For him. "Bingo!"

"You're wrong," I managed feebly. "What made you say that? Some sneaky trick."

"I don't sneak. I *nudge*. I pick, I infer, I listen. Mostly, I listen. For the denials, the claims, the padding, the crap. I never sneak."

"Good for you."

"You like Tarantino?"

"Who?"

"Quentin Tarantino, the movie director."

"He's okay. *Pulp Fiction* was amazing, but it gave me nightmares for a week."

"How about Woody Allen?"

"I liked *Annie Hall*. My parents own the video. I haven't seen many of his movies."

"There was a time when you would have been his dream girl: WASP, bright, restless. Something new of his is opening soon. I'll take you."

I was speechless.

"You can't keep going to the same movies. Different versions, different casts, but the same thing, over and over. Like your music." Something occurred to him. "Maybe you won't go out with me. Would your mother let you? I'll have to ask her."

"I'll ask her."

He doubted it. "Will you?"

"Sure. Why not?" *What was I talking about?*

"How old are you?"

"Sixteen. How old are you?"

That amused him. "Twenty-six. I have a sixteen-year-old cousin. She's nothing like you."

"People tend to be different."

"Not at sixteen. Or so I thought. I could be wrong."

There was a commotion at the front door as my mother arrived, laden, from the grocery store. I rushed away to help her, glad to escape. He stayed behind in the living room but came to the doorway to watch.

"You're early," Mom greeted him, a definite edge to her voice.

He nodded, again offering neither apology nor explanation.

"You'll have to wait." She handed me two heavy paper bags and followed me to the kitchen with the third.

"He's been here for ages," I whispered as we put things away.

"Sneak," she said. "I suppose he's been asking you a million questions."

"Mostly about school."

"You didn't tell him about last year?"

I had to think for a minute. "You mean when I cut chemistry?"

"For two weeks!"

"I didn't tell him."

"This is beginning to infuriate me. If that was Fischer's intention, he's succeeded. We are the most aboveboard, normal family in the world, and being scrutinized like this is making me crazy."

"He wants to take me to a Woody Allen movie."

She was speechless, a rare event with my mother.

"I say let him. We have nothing in common, he'll be bored stiff—so will I—and that will be that. If I don't go, he'll come up with all sorts of stupid reasons why—"

"He's thirty!"

"He's twenty-six."

"How do you know?"

"He told me. One movie, Mom. I can handle it."

She hesitated. "Your father will have a fit."

"I can handle it. If I can stay awake."

"We'll see." Which she always says when she needs time. She went to check on Mark, walking past the living room and Alan Gelber without a word. I stayed right behind her.

Mark was asleep and my grandmother was sitting by his bed, reading. She smiled at us as we came in. It's easy to see where Mom gets her looks, especially when Gram smiles.

"How long has he been asleep?" my mother whispered.

My grandmother looked at her watch. "About an hour."

"He sleeps an awful lot," my mother worried. "He ought to move around more."

"He said he had a long session with the therapist," Gram defended him.

"He sleeps a lot in the *daytime*," I said. "He watches TV all night."

Mom looked disgusted, but Mark stirred, saw her, and grinned, the way he always does when he sees her. She brightened up, bent over, and kissed him.

Gram and I went into the hallway. "What're you reading?" I asked her. She reads some incredible trash, and it cracks me up.

She held it up: a paperback mystery by an old-time movie actress who started writing best-sellers when she couldn't get any more acting jobs. Producers and casting directors are almost always killed off in her books. "I've already figured out who the murderer is, and I'm not even halfway."

Who killed Janine Billings? A little shiver ran through me.

"Are you all right, Cristina? You look tired. And you're trembling."

"I'm fine, Gram."

"Are you sure, dear? I'm going to dinner and the ballet tonight, but I can stay a little longer if you need me."

"Go ahead, Gram. Alan Gelber's in the living room. Just ignore him."

"Who?"

"The researcher for *Weekend Closeup*."

She frowned, glancing toward the living room. "I don't know what your mother can be thinking. When I was a girl, people of substance permitted their names in the paper for births, debuts, marriages, and deaths. Any other mention was considered to be scandal."

I had a flash of the reporters who'd chased me from school. Scandal, definitely.

Gram kissed me lightly. She and my mother are experts at the Near Miss Kiss, used for hellos, good-byes, and numerous things in between. "If you're sure you don't need me, I'll go. Tell Mother I'll call her in the morning."

Mom kept Gelber waiting almost an hour, and it was totally deliberate. I was incredibly relieved, when she told me about it later, to hear that Gelber had not even mentioned Janine Billings. The connection had apparently not been made for *Weekend Closeup*. They wanted us for our dull old selves.

Markie called to tell me about the piece on the five o'clock news, which was repeated at six o'clock, led off by Janine Billings' picture, the same one the Sunday paper had used. That was followed by a tape shot outside my school, edited to show several of the girls in my class arriving at school: Ellie Blair, Neva, Leslie Quinn, and Markie. Markie looked at the camera as though it were a pistol pointed right at her head. The reporter narrating the tape talked a lot of pap about our being "American aristocracy." By the time it was over, the total impression given was one of decadent, filthy-rich airheads and it seemed that Janine Billings had been killed when some gross party game went wrong. It was the stupidest bit of television journalism I had ever seen: mean-spirited, totally lacking in facts or any real research, and spewing all the usual banalities the media reserves for the privileged. The most interesting part for me was seeing Francesca sail past the camera using Ellie Blair as a block. She completely covered her face, and if I hadn't recognized what she was wearing, I could not have been sure it was Francesca. A well-executed dodge. I would have to remember how to do that, just in case.

"That was quite a party Markie had." My mother's voice was thick with sarcasm. The news segment had just ended and a jarringly chaotic car commercial was on.

I could only stare at her. I hadn't heard her come in, I was so into the telecast.

"When were you planning to tell us?" Her mouth was set the way it gets when she is really angry. "I just got off the phone with Ellie Blair's mother, who told me about the police at school this morning."

"Calm down, Mom."

"*Chill out, Cristina!*" She was flushed and furious, as angry as I have ever seen her. "We don't operate like this. Not in this family. I know Francesca's into secrets, lies even. Maybe Markie too. But you have two parents who are here for you, ready to listen, able to take it all in, no matter what it is."

"I know that, Mom."

"Why didn't you tell us this when you came home Saturday night?" Her voice cracked.

"I didn't know about—the murder—until yesterday. And it didn't seem—real, somehow. I kept pushing it away, like if I didn't think about it, maybe it hadn't really happened."

"Why didn't you call from school, tell me about the police

being there? You used to call from school if you got a good grade on a paper. And anytime you had a problem. Always, with a problem."

"I'm sorry, Mom. I should have called." It had not occurred to me to call, and she was right—a year ago it would have been the first thing I'd have done.

"Do the police have any idea who did this frightful thing?"

"Not that I know of. I don't think it has anything to do with the party, anyone at the party, I mean. I think it just happened. She was pretty wild."

"Really." My mother gave me an odd look. "She went to school around the corner from you, lived a few blocks from here. Her mother is a banker, a fine, respectable woman."

As usual, my mother knew more than I did. She could have been any one of you, she was telling me. She could have been you.

"She seems to have been in trouble quite a lot," she went on. "It's hard, when there's only one parent, nobody at home after school. She'd been in drug rehabilitation, but that doesn't always work, of course."

"I'm really sorry, Mom."

"That's not enough, Cristina."

I was staring again because I didn't know what else to say. I wasn't sure what to think.

"I don't know what I'd do if anything this terrible ever happened to you," she said tightly. "This girl has been brutally murdered, a girl your age, someone you knew, even slightly. No matter how you try to distance yourselves from it, you and Markie and Francesca and everyone else who was at Markie's party, you will be changed forever by what happened to that poor girl. You must all deal with it, inside yourselves. Don't push it away; think about it. Face it, the reality of it, the senseless horror of it, the terrible, irrevocable waste of it.

"We've probably seen just a fraction of what may develop with the media. When a crime gets as much immediate play as this one has, it can drag on and on publicly until there's nothing left of it, and not much left of anyone even remotely connected to it. Forget all the gossip about this girl. No matter what was true or what wasn't, she's the victim here. She's dead. We need to focus on the tragedy of her death and stick very closely and completely *together*."

Mom said she might call off Alan Gelber, but the next thing I knew, the housepainters arrived; and the upholsterers, measuring the living-room couches and every other stick of furniture in the "public rooms," as my grandmother calls the living room, dining room, and front hall. Not many members of the public had been around our apartment after Mom had gone back to work. She used to entertain a lot, and not just at dinner with Daddy. She was class mother for years and years at Alex's school, and president of the Parents' Association at my school when I was in sixth and seventh grade. She gave luncheons and teas. Miriam used to wear a pretty black uniform with a stiff white apron and help out at a lot of those parties. I remember them as crowded and noisy, and afterward we always had pizza for dinner.

"I guess we're doing *Weekend Closeup*," I said when she asked me to clean all the "visible silver."

Mom's chin went up. Daddy calls this her "brave front," and she always sticks her chin up when she announces she's going to do something she has serious problems with. "When I tried to discourage this—interview—or whatever they're calling it, Alan Gelber asked me—in that calm, dry way of his—whether I thought we'd been getting quite enough publicity from the Billings murder. Well, I decided right then and there, we have nothing whatsoever to hide. Why should we be so reluctant to go on *Weekend Closeup*? We're proud of who we are and how we're conducting our lives." She hesitated. "I certainly wasn't going to let them portray us as 'not willing to appear on camera.' "

We have a lot of "visible silver," and I think most of it hasn't been cleaned in years. It occurred to me—but I wouldn't mention it—that Gelber probably would have preferred everything left just the way it was, *cinéma-vérité*, warts and all, slightly worn to totally threadbare, tarnished silver, and the chipped gilt frame on Great-Grandfather's portrait. Gelber probably would have found all that charming, but my mother's into pristine. Everything.

I can hardly remember when reporters and photographers weren't lurking around my school. My picture's been in the paper twice, for no reason other than I go to my school and they've somehow figured out who went to Markie's party. It's a bummer, I can tell you. I don't know how really famous people put up with this all the time.

Francesca says they're all over the club scene as well. I was supposed to be grounded for going to Markie's party, but it never happened. Still, I haven't been out since because

Brian's not up to it. We hang out at his house or mine, watching television. It doesn't matter where we are; there's always a mother hovering right nearby. This place is a zoo because my mother's putting so much pressure on everybody to finish everything in record time.

"I told them I'd try to get them listed on the credits," she confided halfway through the renovation madness. It looked as though we were moving. The furniture had been sent out for re-covering, and all the pictures and mirrors had been taken down for the paint job. We had two weeks to do everything before the film crew hit.

Things got so horrendous, I was allowed to go to Francesca's one afternoon to study. I had called Mom from school to say Francesca and I were working on a paper together, which was sort of true. We were actually working on two papers, makeup work, she for medieval history and me for English. I was surprised when my mother agreed, but the noise in the background sounded as if they were tearing down walls.

"What's going on there?" I shouted into the phone.

"Mr. Abernathy is fixing some molding in the dining room," she shouted back. "He's an absolute genius!"

I'm sure my mother had told Mr. Abernathy what a genius he was about four thousand times. She's a pro at getting workmen to achieve miracles for her, and it's a trip for everybody because she totally believes the incredible compliments she hands out, and whoever's getting the kudos believes them too. It works, and I had the green light to go to Francesca's.

I love going to Francesca's apartment. She lives close to our school in a very fancy building where a lot of famous people live. Her mother fought long and hard in the courts to keep it. The famous movie director she may or may not have been married to who may or may not be Francesca's father claimed it was his and he had only "lent" it to her. It is full of antiques and wonderful works of art, but the living room is roped off, like a showroom in a museum. The miniature poodle, Sergei, is allowed in there, but we are not. That always amazes me. Francesca's mother is wildly glamorous, but I wouldn't want to live with her.

And she was still in Europe, or I would not have been invited over.

There is another room in Francesca's apartment that is one of the greatest rooms in the whole world. It's called the library, but it is the real living room. The walls are floor-to-ceiling bookcases, overflowing with all kinds of books; the TV and the VCR are hidden in an elegant cabinet. And if the right section of one bookcase is pressed, it opens to reveal a bar that has a soda fountain at one end. It is a wonderful, magical room, and I have been lucky enough to grow up in it right along with Francesca. When her mother is away, of course.

Francesca opened the bar. "Beer? Wine? A brandy Alexander, perhaps. I make a mean one."

"Diet Coke."

"Cristina, you are such a drag. I'll make you an ice-cream soda. I came up with a really great one the other day: praline crunch ice cream with fudge sauce and Sprite for the fizz. You'll love it."

She set to making it, and the noise of the blender blocked out any further conversation for a time. She emerged from behind the bar with two tall, foamy glasses filled to over-flowing, complete with long spoons and straws. She handed me mine and then collapsed onto one of the overstuffed sofas to devour hers.

I sipped mine and watched her. Something was definitely up. Francesca is stick-thin and determined to stay that way. The only time she pigs out is when she's really upset about something.

She sucked up the last of the liquid noisily and then began to eat the ice cream with a kind of desperation. When her glass was completely empty, she looked up at me. "Don't you like yours?"

"It's great. I just don't want to choke on it."

"It is great. Maybe I'll make myself another one."

"Francesca, I can't stay too long. I'm supposed to bring pizza home for everybody's dinner."

She wasn't listening to me. She was off somewhere else entirely.

"Francesca—what's going on?"

She stared at me. "Gordon's asking me for money again. A loan." She laughed, dryly. "That's all he ever wants from me these days. Sometimes I think it's the only thing I have that interests him."

"Don't be dumb." I had no interest in defending him, but she looked so down. "Tell him what you always tell me—you're broke."

She ignored that as I knew she would. "I should add up what he's borrowed. I wonder what he does with it. I pay, wherever we go together."

"Tell him no."

Her face changed completely. "He'll pay me back! It's just taking him a little longer than he expected to get into something."

He's better at getting out of things, I thought, knowing better than to say it. Gordon Larrimer had been kicked out of at least four prep schools, the first one a very good school, the last a dumping ground for losers like him. Nobody ever got kicked out of the last one, but he'd managed it.

"He's slime," Alex had said. My brother, who never knocks anybody.

"You couldn't lend me a hundred," she asked me now.

"Francesca—"

"Forget it! Forget it! My allowance will clear in two days, and he'll just have to wait until it does. It's not your problem. Don't worry about it."

My soda was so sweet, I was gagging on it. I sipped at it doggedly.

"They've questioned him, you know." She watched for my reaction.

"Who?"

"The police. They questioned Nicky first, and then Gordon. Nicky implicated Gordon, of course."

"How do you know that?"

She threw her head back. "Nicky's such a whining little creep! He always blames Gordon for everything. I'm sure the police were glad to get rid of that sniveling little—Gordon is so much more interesting, even as a murder suspect."

"That's stupid," I said. She was beginning to rave.

She eyeballed me again, those dark-blue headlights flashing and intense. "A lot of people hate Gordon. They're jealous, of course. He's so *hot*."

"Where did he hook up with Nicky Baylor?" Not that it should surprise anyone; they are both losers.

She shrugged. "One of the schools he went to, I suppose." She leaned toward me. "Nicky probably did steal that stuff from Markie's. He has a record."

"Great."

She arched her back against the sofa, staring up at the ceiling with its sculpted iron chandelier. "Why did Gordon let them come with us? He knew I couldn't stand either one of 'em."

"Markie's father has come home."

"I heard. He must be freaking. That's why *I* never have parties." She twisted off the sofa and headed back behind the bar. "Let's have a drink, for Pete's sake!"

"I have to go home."

"Don't be a drag, Crissy! I need to talk. I need . . ." Her voice was suddenly hoarse. She didn't say anything else, just sucked in her lips and sniffled.

"What's *wrong*?"

She poured vodka into a glass, and as she did it, she visibly calmed down. She added ice and orange juice and took a long swallow. "I can usually cope. With guys, I mean. I'm like my mother, after all. My wandering mother. But Gordon. I'm never sure of Gordon. Sometimes he can be such a blank, and then he'll say something—do something—he confuses me. I've never been confused by anybody the way I am by him. And maybe it's me. Maybe I've made him up. I mean, I never seem to reach him, touch him."

"He *is* a blank," I said.

"He's not! You're so smug! You're so secure, with your mom, your dad, perfect Alex, precious Mark. You don't know—"

"Anything." I headed into the hallway.

She was sulking, twirling her glass so that her drink sloshed around inside it.

She stayed where she was while I let myself out. I don't remember walking home. I don't remember crossing streets or paying any attention to traffic lights or traffic. I felt guilty about leaving her there. Francesca, Ms. Unique, Ms. Ultimate Scene Queen, Ms. I'm So Much Cooler Than You Are. The sofa she was sitting on dwarfed her. Once I left, she was completely alone.

Do you know how many people it takes to interview one family on location in their Manhattan apartment? Twenty. Twenty-one, if you count that hyper little man who kept rushing in and out with coffee and sound equipment and more coffee. My mother obviously knew how many were coming. She prepared lunch for about a hundred, and it was all gone before they were, I can tell you.

Alan Gelber arrived first. I wasn't even dressed, but almost; we'd all had breakfast together at dawn or maybe earlier, and frayed nerves were the order of the day. The people with the cameras and the sound equipment came quite soon after Gelber, and several of them seemed surprised when my father asked about some sort of insurance coverage we were entitled to against possible breakage during the shoot.

"Most people don't know about it," the guy who seemed to be head honcho told Daddy. He grinned. "Naturally, the network's not going to advertise it."

"We're always glad when people know about it," the cameraman said. "We don't mean to damage anything, but it happens."

No wonder. I've never seen so much heavy cable, so many lights, so much equipment in one place in my life, and it all appeared to be wired together rather hopelessly like thread in a sewing box so tangled only cutting it apart can free everything.

It was hours before Judy Harley arrived. She was to be the interviewer. I'd seen her once or twice on TV, but she looked much smaller, thinner, and older in real life, and her makeup was very dark and obvious, leading me to believe the natural look I was sporting would not do at all.

"Mom!" I whispered, following her around. She hadn't stopped moving since early morning. "Can I borrow some makeup?"

"You don't need any."

"Mom! This is television! I'll look like a terminal case!"

"You're already wearing mascara and eye shadow. That's enough."

"You're wearing makeup." She didn't a lot.

"You haven't any lines to cover. You don't need it."

"Would everybody step over here, please?" the head honcho called out. "Geri is going to make you gorgeous for the camera."

I giggled and bolted over to Geri, a small, sharp-featured woman wearing no makeup at all and looking as though her hair had been cut with pinking shears. She had a nice smile.

"Sit down." She pointed to one of the chairs Mom had just had re-covered. "You're going to be easy."

When she was done with me, Mom was hovering, and she didn't look too thrilled with the finished product, but she couldn't dwell on it when it turned out Dad was next in line. He looked stricken as he sat where I had just been. He kept his eyes locked on Mom.

"Calm down," Geri soothed. "I'm only going to reduce the shine a little."

"Where's Mark?" I asked my mother.

"They're going to interview him in bed."

"He was up for breakfast."

"I think it's absolutely ridiculous, but Alan insists. He claims it's going to be such a long-drawn-out business, Mark will get too tired. He says he can't risk losing his Star Interview to fatigue."

"I hope Mark didn't hear himself called that." That drew a smile from Mom, but I knew she was feeling manipulated. She'd worked so hard to keep Mark moving, active, healing, and Gelber wanted him languishing like an invalid. It made a much better story.

Alex was incredibly stressed out. He kept disappearing, so every time the lighting man or one of the technical people needed to check out something involving him, I was dispatched to go find him. It wasn't easy, the first time. I tried his room, the den, the kitchen. I finally figured it out, and he was always in the same place after that: Mark's room.

Mark was excited, but not the least bit upset. Alex was jittery and snappish, very non-Alex.

"What's wrong with you?" I asked him.

"Nothing. I hate this."

"Relax. They're sure to find your good side."

There was so much time and flap involved in getting everything set up, the actual interviewing was kind of a letdown. Everything took so long—hours and hours, it seemed—and the lights made the living room unbearably hot. The wires made getting around a hazard to your health. My father kept a low profile, but he was intrigued with the technical stuff—he's like that—and my mother seemed most concerned about feeding people. The hostess. The apartment looked great, even if it didn't resemble our good old comfortable home, and I had to admire the job I'd done on the "visible silver" every time some technician screamed about its glare under the lights. By the time they were finally set up and ready to shoot, most of the "visible silver" was invisible and well out of camera range.

Then, and only then, Judy Harley emerged. She and Gelber were locked in what appeared to be a grim debate for a long time. With the announcement from the head honcho that they were finally set to shoot, she walked abruptly away from Gelber, sat in the chair she'd been assigned, crossed her legs, and was rigidly, irrevocably ready.

Gelber ushered Mom into the chair next to Judy. The crew had rearranged the room for their own purposes, quite drastically in some areas. One corner was crammed with newly re-covered and refinished furniture, stashed there like old rejects.

Mom's interview took the longest, but there was no way to really follow it. Three cameramen worked simultaneously, and Daddy explained it to me: One kept a closeup of Mom, the other kept a closeup of Judy Harley, and the third took "wide shots," which is like watching some loony toon bounce around the living room, with the director ordering, "Pay no attention to him. Please! Never look into the lens—any lens! No matter what he does, take no notice. . . ."

Someone who later turned out to be the sound man was constantly stopping them, complaining about voice levels and outside noise. The crew treated him like a necessary evil and tolerated his troublemaking with a patient resignation they showed no one else.

Dad was next, but by then I was worried about Mom. Her interview took almost two hours, and she looked pale and utterly exhausted when it was over. I wondered how Judy Harley would manage, but she seemed to brighten with Daddy, and she laughed right away at something he said. He has a droll wit and he can be pretty sarcastic, but he's never mean.

They spent almost an hour with Dad, and then they took Alex because I was involved in a hot game of Nintendo with Mark. Mark had become incredibly antsy, cooped up in his room, and even watching TV bored him. I didn't see any of Alex's spot, but it was over in less than half an hour, and he whizzed by Mark's open door and slammed into his own room.

Mom arrived right after that. "You're the final interview out there, then they're coming in here to talk to Mark. It's not too bad, really. I felt kind of sorry for Alex. He was so uptight! He's exactly like your father: so hard on himself."

Judy Harley was having a cigarette in the front hall when I reached the living room. I was dying to join her, but Dad would have busted me on the spot. Gelber escorted me to the proper chair, and the makeup lady fussed over me briefly. I was conscious mainly of the lights. They were hot, and so bright I didn't think I'd be able to keep my eyes open. I was tearing as soon as I sat down in all that glare.

Judy Harley finally came and sat down, watching for her cue.

"You're Cristina," she began, smiling slightly. "You're a year younger than Alex. Sixteen, I guess."

"Right."

"Do you feel your little brother's accident has brought your family closer together?"

The question shouldn't have surprised me, but it did. "I guess so. We're a very close family, though. I mean we've always been very close."

"You were the first to know about it, isn't that so? How did you feel when you couldn't reach your mother?"

I bristled. "I couldn't reach my father either."

"Were you a little panicky?"

"I was very panicky. I didn't know how badly hurt he was. I didn't know anything until we got to the hospital."

"That's a pretty tough spot for a sixteen-year-old."

"I don't think my age made any difference. It would have been just as tough on my mother if she'd been the first to know about it."

"But she was the last to know, isn't that so?"

"She was working. On location. She couldn't be reached."

"And you handled it. Well. Very well, in fact."

"My brother helped. Alex. He knew about it as soon as I did. He's very cool."

"You were both pretty cool. You've handled quite a few tough situations, am I right? With your mother in such a busy job, you and your brother Alex have learned to cope very well."

"There's nothing wrong with that."

"Of course not. You're very independent, I can tell that right away. How does your mother being home full-time now affect that? It must be an adjustment. You were grooved to not having her around for several years."

"It's great. She spoils us."

"You prefer it, then. To her working full-time. You don't find her being at home—crowds you a little? I mean, now she knows exactly when you get home from school. And with whom."

"She always did know. We phoned her at the office the minute we reached home. Always. And we never brought friends home if one of our parents wasn't here. Never." Hardly ever.

"Never. Unusual."

"We've been brought up to have a lot of mutual trust." I spit the words at her. Why did they sound so phony, preachy, defensive?

"Also unusual. Your parents are quite old-fashioned, then."

"Quite."

"And you're happy to have your mother home full-time. Maybe you resented her working such long hours."

"I want her to do what she likes." What crap! I felt like a fried egg under those lights, and I had to sit clutching the arms of the chair to keep from squirming. I despised Judy Harley with a passion I have never experienced before. I wanted one of those blinding lights to explode right into her face.

"What are your interests, Cristina? What kind of music do you like, for instance?"

I hesitated, my rage punctured by the surprising change of subject and focus. "Tracy Chapman, Sheryl Crow, Pearl Jam."

"Did it bother you that your mother ran a lot of parties that made the rich a lot richer?"

My anger was back and setting me off like a rocket. "She ran parties for charity!"

"Sometimes. She also raised a lot of money for some very wealthy men who wanted to become politically powerful."

"She didn't raise it. Her boss—"

"She was very much a part of it. I've interviewed her boss. Your mother was a big producer in his firm."

"You make it sound like they were doing something wrong."

"Not wrong. But the firm is known for catering to the rich and powerful. I just wondered if you had any problem with that."

"If you're waiting for me to criticize my mother, forget it. She went back to work because her three kids go to horribly expensive private schools and she thought it was too much of a financial burden on my father to carry the whole load. Interview somebody in the Board of Education and find out why this city's public school system is such a shambles, people have to look elsewhere—and pay through the nose—just to educate their kids!"

"Your mother went to the same school you're going to, didn't she?"

"That was ages ago, before it was so expensive."

"Your father went to a top-flight prep school and an Ivy League university. Your parents have been into private education for a long time."

"What's wrong with that?"

"Nothing. But it's hardly surprising they send you three to private schools."

"There aren't any other choices in this city."

"Do most of your friends' mothers work?"

"Some."

"Do you feel the ones whose mothers don't work have an advantage?"

"Why? Their mothers aren't home any more than if they had jobs. When a person works, she keeps to a pretty tight schedule. Mothers who don't work can be unpredictable."

"Interesting point. Do you like living in the city? Would life in a smaller, less active place be nicer, do you think? More predictable, perhaps?"

If she was trying to keep me off balance, she was succeeding. "I love living in the city. I cannot imagine living anywhere else. We usually go away for a month in the summer, and I'm always frantic to get back to the city. My mother grew up in this apartment. My grandparents were born and brought up right here in New York."

"Do you think what happened to your little brother would have been as likely to happen in a small town?"

"People have accidents in small towns. If he'd been crossing a busy road in the country, he might have been killed. They don't have a lot of traffic lights to slow drivers down. And I doubt the police and ambulance help would have been there as fast."

She smiled. "A city kid. For sure."

It went on like that for quite a while longer, but it got easier somehow. She asked the questions I'd expected her to ask in the first place: all that junk about drugs and alcohol and sex among kids my age. I'd read so much, written so many papers about all this stuff, I was able to babble on and on about it. Yes, I knew kids on drugs, kids who drank. Everybody I knew did something, except for Alex and Brian and Kate Lovett. Naturally, I didn't get specific.

And when the next question came, I was ready.

"Something very serious happened to you recently." Her eyes locked on to mine. "A young woman in your crowd was murdered."

"She wasn't in my crowd," I corrected, trying not to sound defensive or snobbish.

"Really?" She acted confused, and I use *acted* in the phoniest sense. "She was from this neighborhood, went to school around here."

"She came to a party I went to. It was a big party. I had friends there; I guess she did too." I felt like I was sinking fast.

"Her friend got into a fight at that party."

"He started a fight. He was asked to leave."

"Did he?"

"Finally. And she left with him."

"On her own?"

87**.**

"Yes. She was fine when she left."

"She was killed in the subway."

"That's what I understand."

"Some of your friends have been questioned about it."

No friend of mine. "Have they arrested anyone?" My turn.

"Not that I know of." She almost smiled.

My point.

"How do you personally feel about sex before marriage?"

Hadn't she already asked me that? "I think I'm a little young to take on a really serious commitment. I think that's the most personal decision there is, and everyone has to make it for him- or herself. Drugs, drinking tend to muddy things up, so I don't get into that. It's good to learn as much as possible about all this stuff, so there are no surprises. I'm in no hurry." Brian, hope you're not listening!

That was pretty much it. Judy Harley stood as soon as the lights were turned off and rubbed the back of her neck, wearily.

"Good interview," Alan Gelber said, materializing out of the massive inkblot that was my view after the bright lights went out. "She was pretty tough on you."

I shrugged, not wanting to admit how much she had bothered me. They were dragging equipment into Mark's room, and the focus shifted quickly. I stood in the ravaged living room feeling strung out, wondering what I'd actually said on camera.

Mom was smiling. "You were wonderful. Did you really mean all those nice things you said about me?" She was kidding, but she was pleased.

"You were great, baby." My father put his arm around me. "You looked great, and you handled yourself like you'd done this a hundred times. Alex was so nervous. I hope they'll be quick with Mark."

That spooked us all, so we bucked to Mark's room, which was full of people, cameras, cable, lights. Judy Harley was sitting close to Mark's bed. Her smile was back.

"People have been great," Mark was saying, looking right into the camera. "I guess sometimes it takes the worst thing in the world to happen to bring out the best in people."

Dad and I looked at each other in disbelief. Mark, looking small and pale and ancient with his thick eyeglasses, was having a blast.

"Did you tell him to say that?" Dad whispered to me.

"Are you kidding? He writes all his own stuff."

Something sufficiently terrible has happened in the world, a bloody coup or something in a place previously covered only by *National Geographic*, and the Janine Billings saga is finally off the front pages. It's still floating around the "B" section of the *Times* and page 4 or 5 of the *Daily News*, but it's obvious it's slipping. Every article is just a rehash of old stuff written when it was front-page news.

That doesn't seem to slow down the tight group of snoops who've been hanging around our school since the first news leak. Mrs. Halladay wears an incredible disguise to and from school, and has since the whole thing started.

"It's such irony," she admitted to Neva and me after rehearsal one night as she put on a fake nose, gray wig, and eyeglasses, preparing to leave for home. "An actress is supposed to welcome publicity, any sort of publicity. But—can you imagine how the viewers of *Westport Diary* would feel about the villainous Amanda *teaching* in a private girls' school? Horrors!"

"Have you ever wondered," Francesca had asked me when I repeated Mrs. Halladay's line, "if there really is a *Mr.* Halladay?"

Mrs. Walpole called me into her office a couple of days later. "We haven't seen you at college lab," she said, her eyebrows arching almost out of sight beneath her blue-gray hairline. "You are the only member of your class who hasn't signed up for the next SAT, the medieval history AP, the English achievement. And your grades have fallen below par. What is going on, Cristina?"

Academically I've been having the time of my life, I wanted to tell her. I haven't felt this carefree and nonpressurized since fourth grade.

"I wanted to talk this over with you before I phone your parents. You know, this is your responsibility and yours alone."

Don't call my parents! "I'm sorry, Mrs. Walpole. I'll get organized."

And then a very weird thing happened. Mrs. Walpole, guardian of the strictly correct and admirer—exclusively— of the smartest girls in my school, leaned across her desk toward me in a way I have seen her use only with Leslie Quinn, several of the superbrains in the senior class, and Adelaide Courter, after her father donated a million dollars to the endowment fund. "I realize this is a difficult time for you. If you need to talk, to work things out, well—just come to me. I truly want to help."

As always when I'm confused about something, I went directly to Francesca.

"I thought you were mad at me," she teased. "The way you took off from my apartment—"

"I had to get home." I put the lid on it. "What do I do about college lab?"

"Why haven't you been going?" she asked me.

"You know why!" I glanced around to be sure no one was within earshot. We were hanging out in the junior lounge between classes.

She looked puzzled. "You have to go to college lab, you twit! Otherwise they'll *know*! I am taking every AP and achievement I'm advised to take. It's a dead giveaway if you don't. You have to go through the motions or you'll get nothing but grief." She shook her head. "For somebody as smart as you are, Cristina, you are totally lacking in skills involving subterfuge and deceit. We have to work on those. What else did Windy Walpole say?"

I told her about the "difficult time" speech.

"She's talking about the murder," Francesca translated. That seemed to bother her. "Why should she think you, especially, would be affected by the murder?"

"Are you sure—?"

She nodded as though I should have been able to figure it out for myself. "What else? You're close to me, I date Gordon, he's been questioned by the police—she's madly curious, the old phony! Don't you tell her a thing."

"What do *I* know?"

Francesca thought about that for a minute, then nodded again. "You're right."

There was something about the way she said that that made me want to ask her, What do *you* know?

Markie shuffled into the lounge just as the fifth-period bell rang. She'd been out of school a lot lately, and she looked sloppy, even for Markie.

Francesca got up abruptly.

"We don't have class for forty minutes," I reminded her.

"I have to check something. In the library." And she was gone.

Markie looked at me with a sad little smile. "She can't stand to be in the same room with me. Like it's all my fault. It's all *her* fault!"

I thought she was going to cry again. She cries easily and often lately. She is an absolute mess since the party.

"Come on, Markie. Sit down here. Take it easy."

"Frieda's left, Cristina! I think my father fired her, but maybe she just left on her own. He hired this couple, an ugly husband and wife, and I have to call them Mr. and Mrs. Ender. They're ugly and creepy and they hate me!"

"Frieda—"

"He said she was in charge. He said she shouldn't have let me have the party. He said—"

"Take it easy, Markie." I didn't know what else to say. Firing Frieda was like firing Markie's mother, her real mother. My throat tightened, taking it all in.

"And now I have a bodyguard!" She dissolved into tears. "Ugly, creepy Mr. Ender follows me everywhere; my father's orders. And my father's sending me away to school, starting next semester."

"Oh, Markie."

"I've been in this school since pre-K, and I can't even graduate with my class!"

"Where—?"

"He's choosing. My father. I have nothing to say about it. I have nothing to say about anything, period. Can you imagine, Cris? Leaving *here*?"

I suddenly realized this was home for Markie, and maybe Francesca too, and probably lots of other girls in my school. This was the only constant, the only place they could count on being there, being the same, being safe and secure and there for them.

"Oh, Markie," I said again. Lame. Meaningless. I hugged her and felt the fierceness of her sobs.

She pulled away from me suddenly. Her eyes were a bright, painful red, and her face was wet and blotched from days of crying. "Do you think—your mother—could talk to him?"

"My mother?"

"My father—talks about your mother sometimes. He said once he thought she was the only—real person in the Parents' Association. He said she—reminded him of his mother. His mother died when he was fifteen, but he adored her. The way he talks about her, she could do anything. Maybe if your mother would talk to him . . ."

"I'll ask her, Markie." And she'll say she can't interfere between another parent and his child, but I couldn't turn her down. And maybe Mom would be able to think of *something*.

Markie stuck to me like glue after that, even though we had only one class together. She was waiting for me after

93.

each of the classes I had without her, and when we went to Drama Club, I got my first look at Mr. Ender. He wasn't quite as gross as Markie'd described, but he looked grim and sort of cranky.

The Merchant of Venice is beginning to take shape. Rittenhouse Hall, as our little "theater" is officially known, is on the third floor opposite our neat little gym. Rittenhouse, or Rottenhouse, as it is fondly labeled by the student body, doubles as a ballroom and assembly hall, and it is the scene of upper and lower school graduations, held a week apart early every June. It is a pretty room with a wall of high French windows and several twinkling crystal chandeliers. During Play Week, Rittenhouse Hall is off-limits to all but the cast, techies, and Mrs. Halladay.

Mr. Ender was the only non–Drama Club person present now, and he had obviously been okayed by Mrs. Halladay, because he sat on a chair near the double doors leading to the front hall, the only person on the only chair in the large, empty auditorium. The stage, on the other hand, was mobbed with people: actors, set builders, costume fitters, stagehands, techies like Francesca, who is stage manager, as she has been for the past two years. She is as tough to work for as Mrs. Halladay, according to her hand-picked crew.

And on the very edge of the stage apron, at the corner farthest from all the bustle, sat Luisa Pereira, cross-legged, in jeans and a bulky sweater, and oblivious to the rest of us as she played her recorder. Luisa is another classmate, though a relatively new one, sent from her home in Santiago, Chile, to study music in New York. She has a special schedule at school to accommodate her concert tours. She has played her recorder at Carnegie Hall and Avery Fisher Hall and the John F. Kennedy Center in Washington, D.C. No one knows how Mrs. Halladay managed to work our play dates into her schedule, but to hear Luisa play an Elizabethan ballad now—music that would provide background and atmosphere during the play—was to be carried into the very soul of the play on the wings of her special, super talent. It was amazing to watch everyone react to the delicate beauty of her song, to see people actually become whoever they were supposed to be in the play, accompanied and encouraged by her music. She was awesome, and all that had nagged at me, dragged at me during this long and troublesome day, fell away now and let me focus on Portia and Bassanio and Shylock and the *play*.

It was early in our rehearsal schedule to use music, but obviously Mrs. Halladay knew how distracted we were, how muddled. It worked like a charm.

My mother is constantly at home. I mean, I know I keep harping on this, but before she went to work, she had lots to do out of the apartment. She was a hospital volunteer, she belonged to three museums, she was always running around to lectures and concerts. She even played tennis regularly— ladies' doubles—with a group of her friends on those incredible wood-floor courts at the Seventh Regiment Armory.

Now she's always *here*. She's hovering around Mark, of course, but she seems to have no outside interests. She's always at home when the mail comes. Think about it: The one who receives the daily post knows everything about everybody in the household. Mom knew Alex got deferred for early action at Yale before he did (thin envelope). And she knew I was dragging my feet about eventually applying anywhere.

"You don't open your mail," she accused me, glancing at the pile of college circulars on my desk.

"I'm not in any rush to open that stuff," I faked it. "Have you read where some of those are from?"

"I don't know why Vanderbilt and Tulane wouldn't interest you. Aren't you planning to go to college?"

I froze for a minute, wondering whether Gelber might have said something about our stupid conversation, or maybe Mrs. Walpole had gone ahead and called her, but when she went right on with what she was doing, I knew neither had happened.

She was preparing dinner, which has become a ritual since Mark's been home from the hospital. We'd never had much of a routine about dinner even before Mom went to work full-time. But now we sit down together at precisely the same time, every single night except Saturday, and Mom keeps trying to program that as well.

"When I was growing up," she says a lot lately, "we knew dinner would be served every night at seven, no matter what."

"Your mother had help, dear," my father reminded her, only once. "Having help means keeping to rigid routines."

Mom shook off his argument. "Dinner should be a time for gathering together, reviewing the day's events, renewing relationships."

"Anne," my father cautioned, "please don't get carried away."

I can barely remember the good old days when dinner was a pickup affair and Mom's main contribution was stocking the freezer with meals we could stick in the microwave. Whatever we wanted, whenever we wanted it. It was perfect. Usually we'd fix trays and eat in front of the TV in the den. The dining room was for Thanksgiving, Christmas, and Easter Sunday. Period.

Now the dining-room table is completely set by four every afternoon. It is almost as tough to get out of dinner with the family at seven every night as it is to miss play rehearsal.

We use *napkin rings*, for Pete's sake.

I sat down now at the kitchen table while she chopped and sliced and diced stuff in the Cuisinart, and between processes I told her about Markie.

"Poor child," she said.

"Do you think you could talk to him?" I was very tentative.

"Talk to whom?"

"Markie's father."

"Oh, Cristina—"

"You're the only one he has any use for, Mom. She'll die if she has to leave school! We've been her friends forever. Can you picture what those boarding school bitches will do to her?"

"Cristina!"

"They probably bring their polo ponies with them to class."

"Hardly. When Dad and I looked at boarding schools with Alex—remember when we thought about sending him away for his last two years?—those kids looked like the dregs, punkier and more ragged than even you kids. It was ridiculous, considering what those tuitions are."

"Would you talk to him? Please?"

"I can't interfere."

"She's going to *die*."

"She won't. But it does seem a bit—strong. He's devastated by all that's happened, of course. I can certainly relate to that."

"She didn't have anything to do with the murder!"

"She had that party, Cristina. If she hadn't had that party, the Billings girl would be just another horrible statistic, and none of you would be getting all this ghastly attention."

The telephone rang and I bolted to answer it.

"Don't dilly-dally," she warned me. "Dinner's in half an hour."

The whir of the Cuisinart followed me out of the kitchen as I ran to the den. It was Alan Gelber, although it took me a minute to realize that.

"Hi" was all he said when I answered.

"Hi." I had no idea who he was.

"You haven't forgotten me, so soon?"

"Who's this?"

"Alan Gelber, Cristina. You have cut me to the quick."

"Sorry. My mother's just getting dinner. Can she call you back?"

"I can tell you. I'm just phoning to give you the air date for your segment. We're running it Sunday."

"So soon?"

"Before you guys get any older. It's a good piece. Everyone's impressed. You came off especially well."

"Really."

"And I haven't forgotten about the other thing."

"What other thing?"

"Woody Allen has a new movie opening before Thanksgiving."

Good grief! "I'm really busy now. Exams, the school play, college lab."

"You're in the school play?"

I squeezed my eyes shut.

"What's the play?"

"The Merchant of Venice." That should turn him off.

"Who are you playing—Portia?"

I couldn't say a word.

He laughed, that dry, humorless, pathetic excuse for a laugh. "No kidding!"

"I have to go," I lied. "Thanks for calling."

As soon as I'd replaced the receiver, the phone rang again. He couldn't be calling back. Why had I said I'd go out with him?

It was Francesca, although I nearly didn't recognize *her* voice.

"Something terrible has happened." Either she had developed a terrible cold in the hour since I'd last seen her at school, or she was incredibly upset.

"What?"

"Gordon has been arrested."

"What?"

"He's being kept in some kind of holding cell until a decision is made about bail. His parents will post bail if they set one, no matter how high it is."

Somehow I'd never thought of Gordon as having parents.

"Cris, they think he killed Janine." The way she said it made me shiver. She was shedding. She was shrugging off her semihysteria and working into a trancelike state, which she would probably affect until she regained control over herself. I had seen her do this sort of thing hundreds of times, even when we were little. It is *weird*.

"Do you want to come over?" I didn't know what else to do or say.

"Maybe. I'm going to have to wear a disguise from now on. One of those scumbag reporters asked me about Gordon today, so they've caught on that I'm his girlfriend. Now that he's been arrested . . . "

I didn't hear the rest. I was on overload. I may talk a good game, smoke cigarettes, flirt with a drink once in a while, but I was out of my league here.

And I was going to be on network TV that Sunday. I couldn't deal.

The day the show aired was the fourth straight day of freezing, drenching rain; we'd begun to rehearse *The Merchant of Venice* on Saturdays and Sundays; and I'd taken an English AP the day before, which was baffling to say the least. I was so out of it, I completed the test trying to guess computer patterns with the multiple-choice dots.

Weekend Closeup comes on after the late football game, so its starting time is often delayed, and November 16 was no different. The New York Jets and the Miami Dolphins were slipping around on wet turf at Giants Stadium, playing the kind of football that brought groans and anguished outcries from my father and two brothers. By the time the game finally ended and *Weekend Closeup* came on, I was strugging with calculus homework and had to be pried from my desk by a frantic Mark.

"It's almost on!" He hollered at me from the hallway, twisting on his crutches to get back to the TV as quickly as possible. He gets around the apartment so easily, I often wonder whether his teachers would be as willing to send all his schoolwork home if they knew how agile he has become. I finally abandoned my calculus and trailed him to the den, where everyone had gathered and folding tray tables had been set up. I couldn't believe it. We were dining in front of the television set again, and there wasn't a napkin ring in sight.

The Arts and Leisure section of the Sunday *Times* had an article in it that had been handed around at breakfast. It showed a picture of Mark in bed being interviewed by Judy Harley, and the article was entitled "Super Mom Returns Home." I usually skim through the Arts and Leisure section to find out which of my favorite rock bands are in town as well as the latest videocassette movie releases, but I never read reviews. Somebody named Sean O'Sullivan wrote this one, and it was pretty cool, except that I got a sense he thought women with children belonged at home, period. He obviously isn't a big fan of Judy Harley, and that was okay with me, and he described us as "bright, attractive, closely knit, and loyal." He also said we are "privileged, with a disarming lack of awareness of just how well off they are," which sucked. It made us sound so snobbish and so stupid about it. But what really annoyed me was his wrap-up:

Cristina, the pretty, perky teenage daughter in this family, is also on a fairly fast social track. She attended the party at

Markie Hannigan's home, where Janine Billings was last seen alive before her brutal murder on the platform of the Lexington Avenue subway. It is briefly referred to during the segment, but the otherwise upbeat portrait of a bright, articulate, loving family darkens considerably with its inclusion.

Dinner was the simplest fare since Mom quit her job: spaghetti, salad, Italian bread that had been bought, not baked by her. Things were definitely looking up.

The first segment of *Weekend Closeup* was about some paramilitary group in a rural midwest town where a lot of loonies wear army fatigues and hang around armed to the teeth. The women they interviewed were the scariest. Then came a piece about a doctor who seduced his women patients on a regular basis to "relax" them.

When the third segment started, we were on dessert: vanilla ice cream with Hershey's chocolate sauce, the most awesome finish to the most awesome meal we'd had in months. I hoped it was the beginning of a return to Meals Without Structure.

Judy Harley appeared after the third commercial break. She really looked a lot better on camera than off.

"Anne Morrisey Garcia-Vasquez is a housewife and mother," she began. "She and her lawyer husband live in a large apartment on Manhattan's upper east side, an apartment that has been in Anne's family for nearly forty years. What is remarkable about Anne Morrisey Garcia-Vasquez is not her apartment, or her dynamic, successful husband, an exile from Castro's Cuba, or her three bright and well-turned-out children. Anne Morrisey Garcia-Vasquez has recently resumed being housewife and mother on a full-time basis despite a brilliant and ascending career as a marketing consultant."

Mom was frowning.

"We want to attempt to find out why, when Mom goes back to work and makes a big hit, she suddenly abandons it all for kids and kitchen."

Mom was glaring. The apartment was now on view, a scan shot from the street entrance through the mirrored lobby to the elevator and featuring our doorman, Jerry, who never smiles but grinned like a fool through this entire segment. Finally the camera was in our living room and Judy Harley was interviewing Mom. I thought Mom looked terrific, but she groaned at first sight of herself. Dad led the rest of us in wild applause and cheering until Mom shushed us emphatically.

"You grew up in this apartment," Judy Harley said to Mom. When Mom nodded noncommittally, Harley pursued it. "That's fairly unusual in this city of transients, to find real roots and a sense of stability."

"Many of the apartments in these older buildings have been in the same hands for decades," Mom corrected her, mild but firm. Mom doesn't flaunt her facts, but what she knows she *knows*.

"You didn't work outside the home when your children were smaller." Harley changed the subject quickly.

Mom smiled slightly. "No, but I didn't exactly sleep in."

"Your husband is a very successful corporate lawyer."

"Yes, he is." A proud smile in Dad's general direction.

"What made you decide to go back to work when you did, four years ago?"

"I was getting hooked on *Days of Our Lives*." Mom waited

for Judy Harley to laugh. When she didn't, Mom smiled her little interior smile and waited for the next question. We've all seen that interior smile from time to time. It usually means we're about to find out how far ahead of us Mom is.

"You worked for Fischer Brocknaw before you were married."

"Yes, I did."

"And did he call you or did you call him, four years ago?"

"He called me. We're good friends. We've never lost touch."

"He wanted you to come and work on Senator Lowery's campaign."

"That's right."

"And you did."

"And I did."

"He'd made you other job offers through the years. Why did this one finally convince you?"

"I had the time. The children were all in school full-time. They are very self-sufficient. I was doing some volunteer work, but this sounded challenging. Fun. Political campaigns are very exciting."

"This political campaign was very successful as well."

Mom relaxed, remembering. "Yes, it was."

"Does it bother you that Senator Lowery is currently being investigated for misuse of campaign funds?"

Mom was obviously not surprised by the question, but she was pissed. "Of course it bothers me. Senator Lowery is a fine man and a dedicated public servant with an impeccable record. It is one of the serious drawbacks of public life in this country that it is always open season and the media doesn't care whether accusations are true or based on any truth. Senator Lowery will ultimately be vindicated, and this accusation will no longer be newsworthy. All the fine legislation he has written on behalf of the homeless and the elderly is never mentioned."

The camera had kept Mom and Judy in tight closeup to this point. Now it backed up to include Dad watching Mom, followed by another scan shot of the room, with a brief stop at Great-Grandfather's formal, full-length, rather gloomy portrait. By the time they cut back to Mom and Judy, Mom had settled in and seemed eager for the next question.

"Your children are your first priority," Judy Harley said.

"That's correct," Mom replied.

Suddenly, shockingly, the news footage of Mark lying motionless on Lexington Avenue was edited in: a fragment, a brief, startling clip moving from a long shot to a closeup of his small, helpless, crumpled body, with the chaos of passersby and emergency medical people crowding around a surreal side effect.

Mom looked as though she'd seen a ghost.

Judy Harley's voice narrated over the footage. "Anne Morrisey Garcia-Vasquez was the last to know when her youngest child, Mark, age ten, was hit by a taxicab on Lexington Avenue. Anne was working on location, her husband was out of the country on business, and it fell to their two older children to struggle through this serious crisis alone."

"What about Gram?" Alex muttered. "Gram was there. She dealt with the doctors. We didn't do anything."

Another shift of focus: a closeup of Alex looking grim during his interview segued rapidly into a closeup of me during mine.

"Argh!" I gagged. The TV me looked like a dork. The clip showed the part of my interview where Harley asked me about Mark's accident, and I was pretty stressed out. They shifted quickly to Alex, who looked worried and much less handsome than he really is.

"You took over when your little brother was hurt." Judy Harley looked smug.

Alex shrugged uncomfortably. "It was scary 'til we knew he was okay."

"How did you feel, not having your mother there?"

Alex glared at her as though she'd slapped him. He looked more like his regular self suddenly. "My mother wasn't having her hair done, for Pete's sake! She was at work—off on location. She couldn't be reached."

Judy Harley shifted gears. "You want to go to Yale."

Another shrug. "My dad went there. It's a great school. I applied early and my application's been deferred."

"It's tough to get in if you're from New York. You're competing against the largest block of applicants and the brightest."

"There are a lot of great schools," Alex said. "I'll get into one of 'em, and I'll make them proud to have me."

"All right!" Mark cheered at the TV screen as if Alex had just scored the winning run in a World Series.

"All *right*," my father echoed, grinning at Alex.

Alex looked embarrassed, but we all knew he was relieved his interview was as solid as it was. He'd been dreading this telecast.

My interview was next. It was pretty chopped up, but it wasn't too bad until the end, when she asked me that stuff about Markie's party. They cut from us to that disgusting news footage of Janine's body sprawled on the subway platform with police swarming everywhere. Harley talked over that footage.

"There is a decidedly dark side to this picture of family unity. A girl has been murdered: brutally, publicly, mysteriously murdered. Cristina Garcia-Vasquez seems to take it in stride with all the other high-powered factors in her life: difficult schoolwork, difficult choices to make constantly about drugs and sex, the high price of growing up privileged in a city where everything is available—readily, continually available. Including murder."

If they only knew how out of stride I really was!

There were no other surprises. Mark's interview was as terrific on camera as it had been off, and Dad looked great and was so charming and smart and funny, even Harley was impressed. It showed. There was a brief spot with Fischer, who looked wrinkled and old and acted more of a character than ever. He mugged his way through the whole two minutes: "Anne, come back! *Please!* This is a paid political announcement. . . ."

The segment ended with another clip from Mom's interview, something Mom later told us had actually occurred somewhere in the middle of the taping but that had apparently been picked as potent enough for the finish.

Harley: "You're home now. Full-time."

Mom: "I am. And I'm so busy, I don't know how I ever managed an outside job. I let a lot of things slide, obviously."

Harley: "This is enough for you."

Mom: "More than enough."

Harley: "Even when you read about the world you were

so recently a part of, the movers and shapers you helped move and shape?"

Mom (smiling her interior smile): "You don't have children, Judy. You haven't experienced the wild joy, the exhaustion, the excitement, the frustration, the terror, the constant, unpredictable wonder of being a parent. And having a partner who is every bit as whacked out over all of it as you are, just as hung up on it, just as exhausted from it. It doesn't end when they go to school. It gets more difficult, more complex—for them and for us." She laughed. "People say to me, 'You're not working anymore.' Are they kidding? Try eighteen to twenty hours a day, and weekends. 'You gave up that glamorous job.' You bet. This is the ultimate *adventure*, and I almost missed it!"

The camera moved in for a tight closeup of Mom and froze. It was over. The credits rolled over Mom's face, and fierce applause erupted in our den. Dad kissed Mom, shook Alex's hand, hugged Mark and me, and went back to get really gooey with Mom. We shared some high fives, shouted a lot, laughed at nothing in particular, and then the telephone rang.

And rang.

And rang. Hours later, frantic from the calls, we would take it off the hook and Gram would come down from her apartment, furious at not being able to get through. Even our call waiting was clogged. She told us we'd made the eleven o'clock newscast.

I remember my mother asking, "For heaven's sakes, why?"

"Rita Ramsay said you've made staying home and being a full-time wife and mother sound challenging and fun," Gram quoted proudly.

"That sounds more like you than Rita Ramsay." Mom squinted at her mother.

Gram ignored her and turned to Dad. They get along better anyway. "They showed practically the whole of the last part of the program, where Anne finally put that Harley woman in her place."

Mom looked at me like When did I do that?

"It was an excellent program," Gram pronounced. "You all looked so grown-up and gorgeous." She was obviously very pleased.

There were four or five reporters and photographers outside my building when I rushed out to go to school the day after the show. They trailed me to school, all eight blocks. People on the street—headed for work, walking their dogs, taking their little kids to school—stopped to watch. It was like some crazy sort of parade. I decided I'd have to figure out some kind of disguise to wear home. The Drama Club closet would soon be empty with everyone borrowing stuff to keep these lunatics from recognizing us.

"Who do you think killed Janine Billings?" one of them called after me as we all rushed down the street.

"Did you know Gordon Larrimer has been arrested? Do you think he did it?"

"How well do you know Gordon Larrimer?"

"How well did you know Janine Billings?"

"Do you think drugs had anything to do with Janine Billings' murder?"

I nearly got run over by a taxi as I was crossing Park Avenue, but I kept moving, and the mob scene following me slowed traffic almost to a complete standstill. If there's one thing New Yorkers are more than in a constant rush, it's curious. Let something happen out on the street, like Mark's accident, or a fender bender, or a ridiculous bizarre display like what was trailing after me, and everything stops, everyone stares, traffic lights change and change again, and nobody moves 'til it's out of sight or over.

I was panting by the time I reached school. Kate Lovett was waiting for me in the front lobby. That meant she was missing first-period physics just like I was.

She grinned like she knew some wonderful secret, grabbed my hand, and pulled me toward the stairs. "Mrs. Walpole wants to see you!"

Now what? I staggered as we started to climb. I was exhausted from the record-breaking run I'd just made to get here, and stairs were going to require more breathing power than I had left. "What's up?" I managed to exhale.

"I was sent down to wait for you, dummy. You're late, as usual—how do you get away with this every day?"

"I don't. I do makeup time on weekends."

"You come here on weekends? I didn't know that."

"It's not a hot topic."

"What do you do?"

"Slave labor. Catalogue books for the library, unpack textbooks, enter a lot of boring details into the computer for the office staff."

We had arrived at Mrs. Walpole's small corner office. It has one window that overlooks the courtyard where the lower school takes outdoor recess, weather permitting. It was too cold today, although the torrential downpours had let up for the first time in almost a week.

Kate dragged me in after her like a prize puppy who'd wandered off. "Here she is, Mrs. Walpole!"

Mrs. Walpole was on the telephone, but she looked up and smiled at me. She does not usually smile when I arrive late. I looked around, but no one else was there; she had definitely smiled at *me*.

"I'll call you back," Mrs. Walpole told whoever she was talking to. She hung up quickly. "Good morning, Cristina."

"Morning."

"Thank you, Kate." She dismissed her. "Stop by your physics class to pick up your assignment. I've already explained your absence to Mrs. Henderson."

Kate was gone. I was getting very nervous.

"Sit down, Cristina."

I sat.

"How does it feel to be a celebrity?"

"Excuse me?"

"Your TV show. It was extraordinary. Traditionally we would not have wanted the school's name mentioned, but in this case you were so articulate and mature, you've made us very proud."

I couldn't believe it. "Thanks."

"However—fame carries its own burdens."

Here it comes.

"We've had a number of requests for magazine articles

and television segments about the school. Mrs. Whittaker"—the headmistress—"feels that though this is quite other than our usual policy, it comes at a time when we are launching the biggest fundraising campaign in the school's history. Mrs. Whittaker feels perhaps the publicity might be beneficial." It was obvious Mrs. Walpole wasn't so sure. "But that will be a decision for the Board of Trustees, who are meeting this evening in special session. In any case, that doesn't really concern you. Something more urgent does concern you. That TV show *Star Turn* wants to film a rehearsal of *The Merchant of Venice*. Featuring you in the lead role. Mrs. Halladay has said she will consider it, but she didn't seem very receptive to the idea."

Of course not. *Star Turn* is a mindless, gossipy botch of a program with a sleazy approach and a comic-book mentality. "Mrs. Halladay must hate me!"

"Calm yourself, Cristina. I only wanted to alert you to the situation before you went to rehearsal this afternoon. The television people want to come today, but of course we said that was probably impossible. They were very insistent, so Mrs. Halladay has been asked to reconsider."

I closed my eyes. I was finally breathing normally again, but the memory of that pack pursuing me to school flashed through my mind, so I opened my eyes quickly, glancing around Mrs. Walpole's little office to make sure none of them had gotten up here.

The second-period bell rang, setting every nerve in my body vibrating, and I had to run to get to history class. It was only review, what little I remember of it, but I basically missed it all. So many things were colliding in my head, I couldn't sort out anything. I spent the whole period concentrating on staying calm. This rendered me virtually comatose, but it got me through the morning.

Things improved when I got my calculus test back with an A scrawled across the top, a rare occurrence for me these days. I also handled the nonsense in the dining room pretty well: mostly lower-school kids buzzing around asking for my autograph. This was quickly picked up and mimicked by my slick friends, who held out everything from notebook pages to paper napkins to toilet paper for my celebrity signature. Give me a break.

I was handling all *that* pretty well when Ellie Blair waltzed in with a copy of the *Daily News*. My mother's picture was all over page 5 under the headline

KIDS TOP PRIORITY WITH POWER MOM

The article was mostly a rehash of the *Weekend Closeup* segment, with a one-line reference to the Janine Billings murder, but the lead paragraph knocked me out.

Anne M. Garcia-Vasquez struck a resonant chord for motherhood and homemaking on Weekend Closeup *yesterday, judging from the flood of phone calls the network received after the telecast. Despite loud objections from feminist groups, Mrs. Garcia-Vasquez's eloquent defense of staying home full-time with husband and children brought overwhelming cheers and support from hundreds of women who have been made to feel they are underachievers for choosing to pursue careers that keep them at home.* Weekend Closeup *spokesman Alan Gelber admitted the program had never had such an immediate and enormous response in its ten years on the air.*

I sort of spent the rest of the day in a *zone*, which isn't easy to do with computer lab and advanced Spanish class, where there are only six of us, including Señora Alvarez, heavy into *One Hundred Years of Solitude* in the original *español*.

But I came to with a jolt when the bell rang for dismissal. I hadn't had a minute to figure out what I was going to wear to get past the ever-present press corps, but in any case I had play rehearsal before I could even think of going home.

The drapes had been drawn over the windows in Rittenhouse Hall, and the only light came from the stage, where the set was being built, noisily. Mr. Ender was sitting on his folding chair, which meant Markie was around somewhere, and there were a few other empty folding chairs set up. Odd.

Francesca appeared out of nowhere, as she sometimes does. It occurred to me that she was my only close friend who hadn't called about the telecast. She might have tried, of course, and not been able to get through. She looked weird. Even for her.

She just stared at me. "Francesca!" somebody onstage hollered. She didn't move for a minute, but then she turned and sort of glided away, the way she does when she's acting really stupid.

"Well, Cristina." It was Mrs. Halladay, emerging from the gloom. The Hall is dark when those drapes are drawn, and the stage lights gave the big, basically empty room an eerie glow.

"Hi, Mrs. Halladay!" I'd been spooked all day about this. She hadn't called either, though it would have blown me away if she had.

"We may have to put your name above the title," she said,

smiling her controlled little smile. "You're very photogenic."

"I'm sorry," I said. "About all the commotion."

"It's about time the American viewing public got a good look at a bright, productive family. This country tends to underplay its upper class as though privilege were something to be ashamed of. Mrs. Walpole told you about *Star Turn*."

I nodded, trying not to squirm.

"We're sold out, you know. For the first time since I've been doing these productions, we are completely sold out for every performance. And most of it happened today."

"That's great!"

"I'm going to let *Star Turn* tape your scene with Nerissa in Act Five."

" 'How far that little candle throws his beams'?"

She nodded. "It's brief, it's just you and Neva, and I've told them they're restricted to that single scene. They will be allowed in to shoot it and escorted out when it is over and before we go on with anything else."

Someone approached us. I had to squint into the deep shadows to make out Ellie Blair. She was a techie, one of Francesca's crew.

Mrs. Halladay seemed to know instinctively that she was there. She didn't turn even slightly to look at her. "I'll be with you in a minute, Ellie," which translates into I'm Not Finished Here Yet, and Ellie knew it and moved off quickly.

Mrs. Halladay looked at me intently. Even in that gloom I felt the heat of her authority. "I don't want a lot of talk about this, Cristina. I have instructed those who need to be involved, and I will keep everyone else well out of it. This is a showpiece for the school. They have pressured me into allowing the taping. But you and Neva can handle it. You're good, both of you, and you're mature enough to psych yourselves up for it. Pretend it's opening night. Or closing night. The way you handled Judy Harley, you're not going to have any trouble with a nameless, faceless taping crew from the lowest rung of TV journalism. You're too good for 'em. *Know* it."

Neva was in costume by the time I got backstage. She looked fantastic. She's absolutely beautiful anyway, and when she smiles, it's like a whole flood of lights has been turned on. She was giggling at the moment.

"Do you believe this? The fuss you have caused here, Miss Cristina."

"I'm really sorry."

"Are you kidding? This may be my big break! If I look as good on TV as you do, the movie offers will start rolling in. Then it won't matter whether I graduate or not."

"Naturally, all the movie offers will be for you."

She shrugged. "If you were a big producer and you watched a scene with just the two of us, who would you be interested in?"

"Me, of course. I'm famous already." Which broke us both up until Mrs. Chang appeared, frantic to get me into costume.

It was like magic after that. The corner of scenery we needed for our little duet had been completed, and we took our places in front of it. I was pushed and pulled and pinned into my costume, and Mrs. Chang worked miracles with my hair. The chaos of techies and other cast members melted into the shadows, and Luisa sat on the very edge of the stage at the opposite corner from us and played her recorder.

My mouth was incredibly dry. I stared out into the darkness with widening eyes. The taping crew looked totally out of place in that otherwise empty auditorium (except for Mr. Ender, snoozing near the outer doors). Suddenly Neva's ice-cold hand touched mine. I looked around at her. I wasn't sure where I was, who she was, what we were supposed to be doing.

What was my first line?

"Remember," she whispered, laughter rippling just below the surface, "they're here to see *me*. Don't blow it."

That made me laugh—or rather feel like laughing. Mrs. Halladay suddenly stepped from the black hole that was the backstage wing across the stage, right above Luisa, and she didn't have to glare or anything. Seeing her was like turning on a switch. Or turning off my panic.

She raised one hand, then lowered it, and we began.

Gordon Larrimer has made the front page. His arrest re-opened the Billings murder story like a can of soda that's been shaken up. It spewed all over the papers and the TV news like graffiti on a tenement wall. He's so handsome, he's become a media superstar overnight. He's the guy everyone loves to hate, the boy who has everything, who has thrown it away with both hands. His parents are caught in the media glare as well. His mother is a smallish, forgettable-looking woman who's maybe a little older than mine, and his father has white hair and looks like he's Gordon's grandfather. His mother is the one with the money, from what I hear. She inherited it from her father, who made millions in plastics during World War II. Nobody's quite sure what Gordon's father does, but the picture of them standing with Gordon as he was booked showed the two most forlorn people on the planet. And they don't seem to get along that well. At least, the news footage I watched showed him walking way ahead of her. They could have been total strangers.

I pointed that out to my mother.

"They're traumatized," she said. "Tragedy draws some people closer and splits others completely apart. At this stage of things, it's impossible to judge. They must be paralyzed with the shock of it all."

The news stories tell a bizarre tale: Gordon as a real weirdo, a drugged-out blank who became a dealer and, with Nicky Baylor and Janine, a thief to support his habit. I've never liked him, but I could not believe some of the stuff I was reading about him. It made me wonder what Francesca must be feeling. If all this was true, had she known about it all along? She had said he "confused" her. Maybe she hadn't known.

Nobody answers the phone in my house anymore. We let the answering machine screen every call, and if we want to take it, we pick up. Mostly we let the machine handle things. Mostly it's the press looking for a new spin on the murder. Nuts call or write, praising us, blaming us, threatening us, cursing us out. Most of that is aimed at Mom, reacting to her interview. Most of it is utter garbage.

The phone calls are the worst. It's creepy, not being able to answer your own phone. And somehow, listening to people talk makes them harder to ignore.

"You don't *have* to work, bitch," one woman from Albany said, trying to reach Mom. "I do."

"How do you know what your kids are doing behind your back?" another one asked. She was calling from California, I think. Somewhere out west. "That daughter of yours is the most sophisticated sixteen-year-old I've ever seen. She didn't get that way being a good little girl."

"Nice job, Anne baby!" another woman heckled. "You've set the women's movement back fifty years!"

"Who do you think you're kidding?" another one complained. "I'm a mother. I have *four* kids, and I have yet to experience any wild joy or excitement. You obviously don't do your own housework. That's so obvious! You live in a palace!"

"My husband divorced me for refusing to go back to work," one woman sobbed uncontrollably. We had to replay that tape a couple of times just to understand what she said. "I thought my place was at home with my son, and now that I've watched your broadcast, I know I was right!"

"Her son's probably forty-five," my father joked.

We've installed a caller-ID box. It was that or go the unlisted number route, which we all vetoed. (That would virtually end what was left of my social life.) The caller-ID was Mom's idea. "We have no way of knowing who most of these people are, but at least we'll know where they're calling from. And if some keep calling back."

When Francesca phoned, it surprised me. She hadn't been in school since Monday, and when I tried to call her a couple of times, that stupid message on her answering machine came on: Gordon, doing a turn as an insufferably British butler, prattling on about "Her Ladyship is in the *baaa-th* at the moment, but if you'll leave your name at the sound of the beep . . ." He'd recorded it for her months ago, but hearing his voice now, with her giggling in the background, gave me the creeps. I hung up before he'd finished his silly send-up. When she called me Wednesday night, I got right on the line.

"Oh," she said, "you're there."

I guess she thinks she's the only one who can play hide-and-seek with an answering machine. "Where've you been?" I asked. "Are you sick or something?"

She sighed. "I couldn't deal with school. I may never go back."

She is the only person I know capable of making good on that threat. I frowned into the receiver, feeling a strong wave of the isolation and separateness I'd been dealing with lately. I am still sort of sleepwalking through my usual routines: school, play practice, getting back and forth to school. I've bagged the disguise idea. Unless I buy myself a new winter coat—the one I wear gives me away no matter what I do to my face and hair. And I love the vintage man's overcoat I bought myself in the Village a couple of months ago. It isn't that warm, but it looks fantastically *seedy*.

"Can you come over?" she finally asked me.

How could her mother still be away with all that was going on? "I'm not sure."

"Please, Cris. I'm losing it here. I really am."

"Let me check and see if Mom needs me for anything." I found Mom at her desk, wading through a pile of mail. I told her about Francesca, and in the telling realized how much I wanted to go over there.

"Tonight's that segment on *Star Turn*," she reminded me. "God only knows how they'll handle it now that the Larrimer boy has been arrested. Be home before that goes on, okay?"

"Sure."

"Alex has heard from Yale. Did he tell you?"

"No! What?"

"He got the letter earlier today. He's in."

"Mom! That's sensational! Where is he?"

"Soccer practice. Where else? We'll celebrate at dinner. It'll be nice to have something to cheer about."

There were only a couple of reporters out front when I left my building. I guess the others figured once I came home from school, I'd stay home. These two looked like diehards: a small woman with pasty white skin and hair the color of boot-blacking, and a little round nerd of a man who looked like somebody'd blown him up with a bicycle pump. He had enough camera equipment to photograph two or three major events at the same time, but despite all that baggage, he moved after me as fast as she did, and that was hot on my heels.

"Where y' off to, Cristina?"

We were on a first-name basis, one way. I didn't know or care what either of their names might be.

I couldn't lead them directly to Francesca's, so I made about a dozen detours along the way: a video store, a deli, a pharmacy on Madison I'd never been into before, zigzagging my way to the apartment house where Leslie Quinn lives, where I knew there were two entrances: one obvious, and the other leading to a rear courtyard and a narrow alleyway through to the next street. That's where I lost them, and I ran to Francesca's from there.

She looked unbelievably awful. Her hair, normally the indicator of what kind of mood she's in—crazy, chic, whatever—looked limp and disheveled. There were deep, dark circles under her eyes, and she was scuffing around in bedroom slippers, something I had never seen on her feet before. I couldn't believe she even owned such a thing. She had on what looked like a man's bathrobe, and it had stains and a couple of cigarette-burn holes, but it was her pallor, her haunted look, that really got me. This was either her most dramatic pose ever or the real thing, and I was pretty sure it was real. "Are you alone here?"

"Maxwell's home, I think." Maxwell is the butler. He and his wife live in rooms adjacent to the huge kitchen. I've only seen him when he's chauffeured us somewhere, a rare occurrence. His wife is the family housekeeper, and I've seen her a few times, but I've never heard her utter a word.

We went into the library, and newspapers were everywhere, spread all over the furniture, the oriental rug, the open bar.

"Want to hear the latest?" She scuffed through the mess, kicking a copy of *USA Today* out of her way and picking up another paper to give herself a place to sit. "The autopsy has shown Janine was high on cocaine. Big headline news. Anybody at Markie's party knew that. And the sweatshirt she died in had one of Markie's name tapes sewn onto the neck band. A leftover from summer-camp days, no doubt."

"I didn't hear any of this. I don't read the papers much anymore."

She looked at me wild-eyed. "How can you resist, Crissy?

We're all there, we're all mentioned, every single time, no matter what the article pretends to be about. They rake us over and over like burned-out coals on a barbecue grill. They've even begun to spell my name correctly!" She laughed, the hollowest sound I had ever heard.

"Does your mother know?"

"My mother? *My mother?*"

I was beginning to wish I hadn't come. She was coming apart, right in front of me. I thought about phoning *my* mother.

"My mother has called exactly twice." Francesca tightened visibly at the memory. "We're all over the Paris *Herald Tribune*; we've even made it into *Paris Match*, so she knows, she knows all about it. The first time she called, she gave me a crash course on How to Deal With the Press. She knows a lot about that. The second call was a monologue, totally. She screamed at me for fully fifteen minutes about what all this is doing to *her*. Pity. I've always been so careful not to inconvenience her."

"Why don't you come home with me?" I didn't know what else to say, but I knew I couldn't leave her there. The greatest room in the world was suddenly an overdecorated cage, dirty, restricted, airless. She had liquor on her breath, and I thought I smelled traces of pot. I couldn't be sure, the air was so smotheringly stale, but the heavy drapes had been drawn over the French windows so that no light or air could possibly get in. I was antsy to get out of there.

"I can't," she said.

"Why not? I have that extra bed in my room." I wondered what my mother would say to all this, but I couldn't think of anything else.

She was looking at me as though she had just focused on my being there. "I can imagine how that would go over with your family."

"They won't mind. Alex got into Yale." I realized the minute I'd said it how it must have sounded.

She laughed, a real laugh this time. "Good for Alex." Her face crumpled slightly. "The last thing your family needs is *me*. The first good news to hit since all this misery began, and I show up to spoil things. Thanks, anyway."

"I can't leave you here." I knew she was right about the family's reaction. "I'm supposed to get home to watch *Star Turn*—tonight's our segment—but I want you to get dressed and come with me."

"I have to stay here, Cris. This is the only place where I don't feel like a sideshow freak. I'm okay here, I really am. And I'll call. I'll keep checking in with you. If I get really loopy here, I'll take you up on your offer. You are truly awesome. I guess that's why I called you. I had to touch base with someone I knew would be sane and still in one healthy piece."

She was losing me.

"Gordon's mother calls me about ninety times a day." She was walking me to the door. "It looks bad. It looks very bad for him."

I couldn't believe how casually she said this.

"He had Markie's grandmother's ring. The police found it in his room."

"What?"

"A real idiot, right? Maybe he hadn't had a chance to fence it, but he's unbelievably lazy. It's conceivable he'd forgotten all about it."

"Francesca—"

Her face sagged again. She looked frail and wasted. "I knew he stole sometimes. He's taken things from here. Money mostly, but he took a sterling silver plate once, and I caught him with it. I threatened to tell his parents. I was trying to force him to get help. But he just smiled that sleepy, sexy little smile of his and said, 'They won't care. They don't give a damn what I do.'

"He's nineteen years old. He shouldn't be living with his parents, but he's too lazy to do anything else. And his mother can't say no to him. She absolutely can't."

"Do you think . . . ?" I couldn't finish it.

"Do I think he killed her?" Her eyes misted. "I can't cope with it, but I guess anything's possible."

"Oh, my god!"

"If you ever repeat that, Cris, I'll deny I said it."

"Thanks a lot."

"You can't imagine repeating it now, but who knows what will happen before this all finally ends? The police have already had me in to give a complete accounting of the night of the murder."

"Because Gordon was with you."

Her eyes hardened, but she said nothing. "You're going to miss your program." She dismissed me. "Maybe I'll drag myself to school tomorrow. Thanks so much for coming over."

I planted my feet and eyeballed her. "Gordon wasn't with you."

She tried to smile and had to settle for a shrug. "Believe what you want." Her voice was as thin as thread.

"And while we're talking about this, you knew Janine

pretty well, didn't you?" Neva's remark had stayed with me like an aftertaste.

Francesca was zoning. She sighed a little and glanced toward the library, like I was taking too long to leave.

"How'd you know Janine?" I didn't really want to hear this, but something drove me. "Come on, Francesca."

She straightened slightly and faced me. "Janine provided *services*. Everyone knew Janine."

I ran all the way home. It was dark and getting very cold, but I was trembling from the inside. Until now I hadn't really focused on what had happened the night of Markie's party. I couldn't shake the image of the news photo of Janine Billings' body, covered by a sheet, a wide pool of blood circling her corpse.

I'm a kid, for Pete's sake. I'm only sixteen. I'm a virgin. I brag about the A List and I hang with the cool crowd, but I'm totally bogus. I'm not so cool, and that's the hard fact of it. I do stuff without thinking, I screw up a lot, and somehow, because I don't whine and cry when I get into trouble for it, people think I'm cool. I learned a long time ago, the less you say, the less you'll eventually have to explain. It makes people think you're smarter than you really are. I know people think I'm stronger than I really am.

I was finally home. I went straight to my room and tried to stop *shaking*.

My mother found me half an hour later, sound asleep at the foot of my bed, huddled into my coat as though I were lying frozen in a snowbank. She woke me gently.

"Are you all right? Do you feel all right?"

"I'm fine," I lied.

"You're not fine. Talk to me, Crissy."

"Is it time for *Star Turn*?"

"Showtime!" my father bellowed from the den, perfect timing.

"Come on, Mom!"

"You're going to talk to me," she insisted, trailing me down the hall. "Now, later, you're going to tell me what's weighing on you."

I was psyched to see the tray tables set up again for dinner. Mom's Structure was certainly coming unhinged. The airheaded blonde who hosts *Star Turn* was babbling about what to expect on tonight's show, and then suddenly there was a closeup of Neva and me in costume. I looked a lot better than I had on *Weekend Closeup*, thanks to Mrs. Chang's miraculous hairdressing skills and some heavy stage makeup. The closeup was a still that dissolved to an exterior shot of my school, the news footage of several of my classmates going to school, which dissolved to an exterior shot of Markie's apartment house, and finally the inevitable shot of Janine Billings' body on the subway platform. All this had a voice-over narration by the airhead that I couldn't seem to grasp, it was so moronic, but I caught a few phrases that were becoming total clichés, like "Manhattan's young royals" and "Is murder their latest party game?" The shot of Janine dissolved to a recent closeup of Gordon, and even though his hair was mussed and he needed a shave, he still looked incredible. Blank, but incredible.

"Not since Robert Chambers murdered Jennifer Levin in Central Park—the infamous 'Preppie Murder' of the 1980s—has the rarefied world of the elegant upper east side been as severely shaken," the airhead continued. "Life goes on for these young hell-raisers. They go to class, do their homework, take their extracurricular activities very seriously. Judge for yourself: Here's a scene from their current production of Shakespeare's *Merchant of Venice*, to be presented just after their Thanksgiving break."

At last our little scene, brief and not at all bad. The camera moved in from the middle of the auditorium, focusing on Mrs. Halladay (who kept her face well hidden), and Luisa, playing her recorder, before closing in on Neva and me. Our voices could be heard throughout, speaking our lines with the crisp diction Mrs. Halladay insisted on, but with absolutely no timbre. I knew for sure that would be her criticism tomorrow. We were flat; there was no denying it. I was surprised Neva wasn't better. She must have been as nervous as I was.

"Pretty impressive stuff," the airhead critiqued when our scene was over. She was back on camera, smiling her perfect smile. "If Gordon Larrimer is indicted and goes on trial for

Janine Billings' murder, attorneys for both sides should be aware what well-trained and talented young actors they have for prospective witnesses. From Shakespeare to swearing in a court of law, these kids can be very convincing. The question is, will we ever know for sure whether they choose also to be truthful?"

I was livid. "What's that supposed to mean? Does she think we'd lie under oath? For Gordon Larrimer?"

"For anyone," my mother amended. Her voice was low and granite hard. "Turn it off, please, Alex. I'm sure there's nothing else we'd be interested in on that program."

Alex turned off the set. He had come in just after the telecast had started, delivering the pizza we were now devouring for dinner.

"I propose a toast," my father said, raising his glass of beer. "To our talented children: Alex, Class of Two Thousand and Two at Yale—"

We all raised our glasses and cheered. Alex grinned like he still couldn't believe it. "Thanks, you guys. For putting up with me all the time. And believing I'd make it when I didn't."

More cheers.

"To Cristina," my mother went on with it. "For a brilliant performance."

"To all of us!" Mark shoved his glass up so fast, half his soda slopped over and ran down his sleeve. "We're the greatest!"

Laughter all around.

The phone rang. We all stared at it, but nobody moved.

Ring, ring, ring, ring. Then the answering machine clicked on, and Mark's was the Voice of the Week: "You have reached 555-9904. Please leave your name and a brief message after the beep. Thank you." No names, no promises.

We all sat there like idiots, watching the machine as if it might suddenly crank out a picture of whoever was calling.

"This is Alan Gelber," Alan Gelber said, his voice as mechanized as the answering machine. "Cris, I'd like you to call me. My office number is 555-8800, extension 488, or, after seven P.M. at home: 555-0876." A pause. "That Woody Allen movie is opening at Cinema One." Another pause. "Call me." Quickly. Irritably. Feeling like a wind-up toy, probably, because that's how I always feel talking to machines.

"Whoa!" hooted Mark when the machine clicked off.

Living like this is unbelievable. Your whole life is out there for everyone to watch and listen to.

"And that, ladies and gentlemen, is why we were picked for that golden moment on *Weekend Closeup*." Alex, being a jerk.

"What Woody Allen movie?" my father wanted to know.

I shrugged.

"Are you going?" Mark persisted.

Another shrug.

"Of course not!" My father, glaring at my mother as if it were *her* fault.

"He's only twenty-six," Mom said. "I know he looks older."

The phone rang again, fortunately, and it was Gram, who always leaves abrupt, angry messages like "Call me!" so Mom ran into her bedroom to call her back.

"So, Alex," Mark chirped, determined to get the party back on track. "How does it feel to be a Yale man?"

Alex's grin had become a reflex reaction to the word *Yale*. "Fantastic, champ. Now I can burn all those other applications." It was obvious the reality of the whole thing was just now sinking in.

"When Mom's off the phone, you should call that Gelber guy back," Daddy said. "Where'd he get the idea you'd go out with him?"

"It's just a movie, Dad. He thinks I'm incredibly narrow-minded."

"Really." My father pursed his lips.

"I can't stand him." It was hard to take any of this seriously, yet I was sort of flattered Gelber actually had called.

Mom came back. "Fischer called Mother," she sputtered. "He absolutely despises answering machines, and anyway, I haven't returned his last few calls, so he phoned Mother and asked her to have me call him. He is impossible!"

Dad's sulk deepened. He's never been crazy about Fischer, and he blames him for the whole *Weekend Closeup* mess. "What does he want?"

"Who knows?" Mom caught on to Dad's black mood. "Who cares? What gall, bothering Mother. And she loved it. He flatters her shamelessly!"

I phoned Gelber from my room. By that time he was home. He picked up after one ring; what a dork.

"I wasn't sure you'd call back," he said.

He always makes such a federal case out of everything.

"Cris?"

"Yes."

"When do you want to go?"

Never. I was sort of flattered he'd phoned and all, but that was it. I couldn't say I didn't go out weeknights because of school, like some ten-year-old. "Friday's okay." Dad would freak. He was treating me like a ten-year-old.

"Super!" Was that surprise in Gelber's voice? "I'll pick you up."

"I'll meet you there."

"Parents don't approve?" He sounded delighted.

"No," I lied, wondering why I was doing this. "It's just easier. I'll be coming right from play practice. We run really late on Fridays."

"I can pick you up at school."

Wonderful. The paparazzi would have a field day. And then the whole world would know, including and especially my father. "I'll meet you at the theater."

"Okay. Fridays—" He was rattling paper. "Fridays it goes on at seven-thirty and nine-thirty. Nine-thirty, I guess."

"Fine." *Yuck.*

"It'll be mobbed—first weekend and all. I'll get there early and buy the tickets."

What? My father did things like that. This was maybe the dumbest thing I'd ever done, but I was so pissed at my father for saying I couldn't go, I went ahead with it.

After I hung up, I sat staring at the telephone, wishing I could take back every word I'd just said to him, wishing I could erase the whole fact of him like deleted text in my computer. I didn't even hear my mother come in.

"I want to show you something."

I jumped at her first word.

"You were miles away," she smiled, handing me a small sheet of paper. "Read this when you have a chance."

My mother is constantly giving me stuff to read: articles

from the daily paper or magazines. She's done it to all of us for years, and she's really cool with her clippings. Most of what she hands out is pretty interesting.

This was not a clipping. It was a letter. I turned it over to read the signature: *Helena Billings*. Billings. Janine Billings.

Dear Mrs. Garcia-Vasquez,

I have tried several times to phone you, but to no avail. What I have to say cannot be said into an answering machine.

I was very impressed with your television interview. The portrait of your family was moving, enviable, quite extraordinary.

It was my daughter, Janine, who was murdered in the subway three weeks ago. So much has been written and telecast and discussed since then about Gordon Larrimer and Nicky Baylor and your daughter and her friends, and so piteously little has been said about Janine, except in a slighting, disinterested, derogatory way.

Janine was my only child. My husband and I have been divorced for years, and Janine hardly knew him. She didn't interest him either.

When Janine is mentioned in the sickening media blitz of all this, she is dismissed as "wild," a "hanger-on," even by one particularly heartless columnist as a "camp follower."

Janine was not a pretty child like your daughter. She had a plain little face, stick-straight, flyaway hair of no particular color, a chunky little figure, and skin problems. She bit her fingernails and wound one strand of hair so incessantly, it stuck out from her head no matter what she slicked onto it to keep it down.

I'm a banker, an executive with a big commercial bank, and I've worked hard to get where I am. I have been Janine's sole support for her entire life. I work long hours, and I have to travel a bit. Janine was a quiet girl. I didn't realize how constantly alone she was. I struggled to put her in a good school and to keep her there. It wasn't enough. It wasn't nearly enough.

Janine had no friends, it seems. I assumed she did, but she was never allowed to bring people home because I wasn't home. She brought a lot of people home, as it turns out. Some of the crueler news stories suggest she ran a brothel in my apartment. I may never know the whole truth, although I'm trying to find out what I can, too late to help my daughter. I'm not sure I ever want to know it all.

I do know one thing: Gordon Larrimer is evil. He is handsome, he is the darling of the tabloids, but the fact is he is a drug dealer, a thief, a seducer, and thoroughly evil. Nicky Baylor is as pliable as Janine, vulnerable, easily manipulated. They were completely obsessed and dominated by Gordon Larrimer. They did his dirty work for him, took terrible risks so he wouldn't have to take them, fenced the things he stole, dealt the drugs he passed. There was nothing they wouldn't do for him. And Janine died because of him. I don't have proof he killed her, but he was responsible for her death, I am sure of that.

I don't know why I am writing to you. You are the sort of people I envy, even resent. You have it all. But you seemed, on that TV show at least, to be a caring and kind person. I guess I just needed to write this to someone and, like Janine, had no one. Forgive me for imposing on you.

*And beware of Gordon Larrimer. I read that your daugh-
ter's best friend is his girlfriend. I hope your daughter has
nothing to do with him. Ever.*

*This does not require an answer. If you read it through,
I'm grateful.*

Brian phoned while we were finishing dinner. I hadn't
talked to him in *days*. I'd begun to worry whether he would
call.

"How's your arm?"

"Okay. The Murray Hill game's coming up, and I haven't
been to practice since I got hurt. I hope they'll let me play."

"Of course they'll let you play. You're the goalie. They've
been struggling without you."

"Wayne Coogan's been goalie since I got hurt."

"They'll let you play, Bri. I've got Drama Club—what else
is new? I'll try to get there for part of the game. The end,
probably."

"Larrimer's in deep trouble." Brian sounded like he found
that hard to believe.

"He deserves to be."

"Really? You heard something I haven't?"

"No. But he's a creep. He could have done it. Easily."

"Geez, Cris! You believe that?" He was shocked.

"I don't know what to believe."

"Don't hang the guy 'til you're sure he's guilty. I mean,
I'm no fan of his, you know that. But whoever killed Janine
Billings nearly cut her head off! You think Larrimer could
have done that?"

Something kept me from mentioning Mrs. Billings' letter.

———

I phoned Francesca much, much later to check on her. I was just about to go to bed, in fact. Her number rang about ten times, and I figured she'd gone out somewhere and forgotten to set her machine. I was hanging up when she answered.

"Gordon?" She trilled his name.

I wanted to hang up in her ear, but I didn't.

"Gordon? Darling?"

"It's me, Francesca."

"Cristina!" She laughed uproariously. She was either tripping out or things had changed dramatically since I had left her in despair a few hours earlier. "Oh, I'm *so* glad you called!"

"Do you get a lot of calls from Gordon these days?" I don't do sarcasm well. "Has a phone in his cell, does he?"

"He's out, Cris! Free! Well, not exactly free free, but out on bail and hopefully on his way over here as we speak."

I had a nightmare image of Francesca in her crummy bathrobe with Gordon standing over her and blood everywhere and then she had no head.

"Cristina? Are you still there?"

"When did all this happen?"

"His mother knows someone who knows someone else. Strings were pulled, bail set and paid, and—"

"He's coming there? Now?"

"As soon as he can. Oh, Cris, I feel like this is our first date or something! I'll call you later, okay? I haven't quite pulled myself together, and you remember how lovely I looked when you were here earlier."

Bathrobe . . . blood . . . beheaded . . .

"Be careful." I had to say it. I felt like calling the cops.

"What are you talking about? Aren't you glad he's out? Why do you sound so morose? Anyway, I really can't talk now. He'll turn on his heel if he sees me looking like this! I'll call you later. Maybe tomorrow. I might even go to school, unless he sleeps over. I actually think there are restrictions attached to this bail business, and he has to stay some- where very specific, like home with his parents. I'll take him any way I can get him! Cheer up, Crissy! Be happy for me!"

Be careful . . . for some reason I thought of a word game we used to play—constantly—when we were in fifth grade. It was supposed to build our vocabularies. Willful, whimsi- cal, wacky Francesca . . . frisky, flippant, fragile Francesca . . . sarcastic, sharp, scared Francesca . . .

Be careful!

Neva's opinion of our *Star Turn* appearance was brief: "We *sucked!*"

Mrs. Halladay murmured something about being glad we had sold all the tickets before *Star Turn* aired, but everybody else liked us. I was getting quite good at being gracious in response to kudos and compliments. I was maybe even be- ginning to believe some of them. But not to worry. Your real friends always bring you screeching right back to reality.

"You were great," a little fourth grader told me breath- lessly. "I'm never allowed to watch *Star Turn*, but Mummy let me because you were on."

"You looked beautiful," Amanda Garrison gushed. She is a sixth grader, but she dresses and makes herself up like a thirty-year-old. *She* is beautiful, under all that pricey blush and lip gloss.

"Who were you supposed to be?" Reenie Dumont cracked. "Emma Thompson?"

"You ought to wear your hair like that all the time," Ellie Blair said. "It isn't really you, but it's gorgeous."

It was all over the papers about Gordon getting out on bail, with a *Times* editorial about double standards for wealthy murder suspects, implying Gordon received very special treatment because of his wealthy mother's friends in high places. Francesca wasn't in school the day after he got out, but she showed up on Friday. She had on layers of her weirdest clothing—she looked like a walking thrift shop—and her hair was spiky and wild and her eyeliner heavy. She was definitely dressed up and ready to be on display. I was sure flashbulbs had popped all over the place when she arrived outside school. The army of reporters and photographers had ballooned in the past couple of days, but a real mob now camped outside Gordon's town house, several blocks down and east. It had been on last night's news, there were so many, but everything about Gordon made headlines these days. The pack pursuing us never mentioned Janine or Markie or anyone but Gordon.

I was in the junior lounge cramming for a quiz in poetry when Francesca appeared. I hadn't seen her all day except at a distance and on the fringe of the crowd surrounding her. She flopped down beside me. She looked slightly peculiar and she couldn't seem to sit still. She fidgeted with the many layers of clothing she wore, twisting around to check out the room and whoever else was in there, and sighing as though she were completely wiped out.

"How's Gordon?" I figured I might as well go for it.

She twisted back toward me stiffly. "He's fine. He's really amazing. You'd never know anything was wrong."

"He has to be glad to be out."

She nodded several times, canvassing the room again. I wasn't sure she'd heard me.

"Who are you looking for?"

Back to me, sighing and leaning up against the beat-up old couch, she seemed finally to relax. "Hal Bregman is going to defend Gordon. He's the absolute best, naturally. Gordon says he looks constipated." She laughed, but it was totally forced. "I warned him not to piss him off. His fee will be staggering, in any case." Another sigh.

"Am I keeping you up?"

She glanced at me as though I'd lost it. "Have you ever heard of Hal Bregman?"

"No."

"He's the absolute best."

"Naturally."

Now she was with me. She shot me a sideways look I know very well. "You think this is funny."

"Not at all. Do you still think he did it?"

She stiffened. I thought she might jump up. She stayed perched on the very edge of that saggy couch and gave me her most withering look. "I never said that, Cristina! I don't think he did it! Of course he didn't do it. What's wrong with you?"

I put up my hands defensively. "My mistake. What's he going to do now?"

She made a face. "His parents have to know where he is

at all times. And my mother has come home. Last night. Can you believe it? I've hardly seen her, of course. She always sleeps for about a week when she's first back from Paris."

I now knew why she'd come to school. "We've missed you at rehearsals."

She threw her head back and laughed heartily. "I watched *Star Turn*. It was terrific!"

A group arrived from volleyball practice and swarmed around Francesca, so I slid off the couch and went to the library.

Neva found me there. "I've been looking for you all morning," she complained. "I brought my stuff, but I wanted to double-check with you, 'cause you're impossible to reach on the telephone. Is it okay if I stay with you 'til we're done with the play?"

Neva has stayed with us for the last weeks of rehearsals and the entire run of the play since sixth grade. She lives too far uptown to go home after our late rehearsals, which would start today, and my mother insists she virtually move in with us for those three weeks. I was surprised she hadn't already talked it over with Neva's mom, a head nurse at a big city hospital and one of my mom's great friends. She usually does. Nothing was normal anymore.

"Cristina, did you hear what I said? You're *spaaa*-ced out today!"

"I hear you, and of course we're expecting you." I would have to remember to call Mom and remind her. We had a code for family calls: three rings, hang up, and try again immediately. "Sorry things are so screwy. Your bed awaits." In my room. The other twin.

"Great. I'll phone my mom. She'll be relieved."

"Gee, Neva. I'm really sorry your mom was worried."

"Don't sweat it. She's so glad her baby missed Markie's party, she doesn't fuss about anything."

Going to a school like mine does have some great perks. Like Playgoers, a spinoff of Drama Club that gives the kids who sign up for it good seats for at least four Broadway or off-Broadway shows a season. Mrs. Halladay arranges everything, including chaperones for each outing, usually a mix of parents and teachers. She has great contacts and knows what's cool.

Art history is taken very seriously as well, and we go on field trips to the many museums in the city on a regular basis, visiting the Metropolitan most often. It's closest and has so much to see, I doubt I'll cover it all in my lifetime, much less my school career. We bitch and moan a lot about going, but everyone really likes it.

I bring this up because we were scheduled to go to the Met that Friday afternoon, and Miss Delmar and Mrs. Walpole were conferring in Mrs. Walpole's office about how best to avoid the pursuing press. They were bound to follow us right into the museum. We hung around outside Mrs. Walpole's office, trying to guess whether or not they'd call the trip off.

"Maybe we'll get out early," somebody said hopefully.

"Dream on," Ellie Blair dismissed it. "Miss Delmar will probably show slides in the studio."

Ellie was a talented artist, Miss Delmar's star pupil, which made her the resident expert about everything to do with art.

"Oh, they won't call the trip *off*, will they?" That was Francesca, making one of her entrances.

"What makes you so anxious to go to the museum?" I asked her.

"I don't care, of course. But we can't let those newspaper people rule our lives. And I thought we were going to see the new American show."

"We're supposed to," I agreed.

"I'm frantic to see that!" She glanced toward Mrs. Walpole's office irritably. "They can't cancel for such a silly reason."

I smiled. "Getting into the fanfare, right? It's kind of a trip, being a celebrity."

She glared at me. "I loathe it. But I'm not going to change any plans to avoid those people. They're not going to trail us around the museum."

"Of course they will."

"Well, they'll have to pay to get in; that should slow them down. We'll sail through on our school passes, and they'll be hard-pressed to track us down."

"The American show is open to the public, Francesca. It's the big attraction over there right now. They'll figure that's where we are."

Miss Delmar and Mrs. Walpole emerged. Miss Delmar is tiny and birdlike, with frizzed, flyaway hair and constantly fluttering little hands. Standing next to solid, matronly, blue-haired Mrs. Walpole, she looked like a hummingbird.

"We've rescheduled today's outing," she said. "There are so many reporters outside school at the moment, it would be foolhardy to try to go to the show, and inconsiderate to the general public, who would be distracted from enjoying the art by the commotion we caused. Cristina, I haven't been able to reach Mr. Perlingham on the phone, and I don't trust that assistant of his. She doesn't always give him his messages. He'll be waiting for us, so please go over there now and give him this note from me." She handed me a sealed envelope. "As for the rest of you, please follow me to the studio. I have some very interesting slides."

Groans all around, as I headed for my locker to get my coat. I wasn't aware of Francesca chasing after me until I was spinning the combination lock on the metal door to my locker.

She was ballistic. "I'm supposed to meet Gordon over there!"

"At the museum?"

She nodded. "I told you, my mother's come home, so we can't go there. His mother volunteers at the Met two days a week, so we figured he could go over there with her, and we'd meet."

I pulled on my coat, waiting for the instructions I knew were coming right up.

She clutched my arm. "We were to meet near the Tiffany windows. The American show is across the courtyard and upstairs from there. You know where I mean, don't you?"

"Francesca—"

"You have to do this for me, Cris! Just tell him I can't get there. He'll understand. Will you do that for me? Please?"

"Okay. I'll deliver this note, and then I'll look for him."

She closed her eyes and exhaled with relief. "He'll be there. He'll be right there. Near the Tiffany windows. You know where that is, right?"

"Yes, Francesca." I wasn't thrilled about this, and I didn't care if she knew that.

"You're an absolute angel, Cristina! I'll never forget this!" And she rushed off in the general direction of the art studio.

I left school by a side door, which led into the little courtyard where there was a locked gate that the custodian, Harold, opened for me. This brought me onto the sidewalk closer to the corner and the entrance to the park by several hundred yards. The media group watching the school's main entrance had their backs to me, and I walked as quickly as possible around the corner and out of their sight, half expecting the whole time that one of them would spot me and alert the others, and the race would once again be on.

But that didn't happen, and I reached the museum quickly, awed as I always am by that grand entry, the pyramid of steps leading to the massively elegant building that so gracefully dominates several blocks of upper Fifth Avenue. Three giant banners flapped in the icy afternoon wind, one announcing the show of American art we'd been scheduled to see, and the other two heralding a touring exhibit of Asian art and something special in the Costume Institute. The guaranteed air of excitement and discovery I always feel at the Met was especially strong today as I entered the huge rotunda, but my customary rush at just being there was rubbed raw by the prospect of meeting Gordon. I felt sneaky, sly, conspiratorial. My parents would be furious and totally disapproving; I was certain of that.

But there was something else as well: a titillation fed by curiosity, perversity, whatever. I tried to push it away, but I knew without any doubt I was madly psyched to see Gordon Larrimer.

I had to deliver my sealed letter first, and Mr. Perlingham wasn't in his office, wasn't in the gallery where his rather grumpy assistant said he would be, wasn't in the restoring room where the gallery guard thought he'd been headed; and I ended up back in his office wondering why I hadn't left the note with his assistant in the first place. Somehow, the way Miss Delmar had specified handing the note directly to Mr. Perlingham, plus his assistant's reluctance to have anything to do with it, caused me to persist in what was a totally bogus chase around that vast building.

He entered his office right behind me, an elderly man with a fringe of white hair, quite tall, very stooped, wearing a dandified suit with a vest and a gold pocket watch, which he toyed with constantly. His assistant introduced us, and he took the note from me.

"I had a feeling you wouldn't be able to come," he muttered, as much to himself as to me. "Incredible how often these things become unmanageable."

I didn't know if he meant field trips or our current crisis with the press. He kept moving into his private office, which looked from where I stood like a complete disaster area of books, papers, photographs, and framed canvases, the latter leaning against his large desk and the single chair facing it like a lot of really pathetic rejects.

"Is there something else you wanted?" his assistant asked me as I stood there, staring after him.

She was really rather rude, I decided, hurrying out of there. Why was I so jittery? Why did everything rattle me? Then I knew. There was something else I had come for. I had to find Gordon Larrimer.

At first I thought he hadn't come, and then I realized he wouldn't be standing around, waiting for a crowd to gather. The Met is always mobbed, and the American Wing is one of the most popular parts of the Met. Tired feet get rested in the courtyard facing the simulated facade of a Federal mansion, filled with period rooms decorated with period furniture and antiques. The Tiffany glass windows face the facade from the opposite side of the skylighted courtyard, tucked neatly into an area made cozier and less visible by a series of partitions and a centerpiece of three fluted columns.

I hope you're impressed. I've been coming here on school trips since I was five years old.

When I rushed into the area, getting panicky about the time since it had taken me so long to track down Mr. Perlingham, I saw two kids wrapped around each other under one of the bronze stairways and wondered instantly whether Gordon might be the male member of that duet. Add another charming layer to this already sickening mix. But I quickly realized I knew neither participant, and I kept scanning the long cloistered walkway for Gordon.

He found me, as it turned out. "Hi, Crissy." He had come up behind me just as my frustration was kicking into high gear.

I whirled around at the first word. Gordon has a deep voice and he sort of murmurs everything. He probably thinks it's sexy, and it probably is for a lot of girls. Not me.

Gordon is very dressy, as I've said before. He normally looks like something out of *The Great Gatsby*. But there, with one of Louis Comfort Tiffany's most elaborate multi-colored glass panels framing him from behind, he looked bland and ordinary and like a million other people. I had to stare at him for quite a while to be sure it was him. I wondered if Francesca had had a hand in this truly amazing transformation or whether the nightmare he was living through had taken a colossal physical as well as emotional toll.

He grinned, picking up on my astonishment, and he instantly became Gordon. I almost warned him not to smile, but I did look around to make sure no one else was watching.

"Francesca won't be coming," I blurted. "Our field trip was canceled because of the media frenzy. I don't have to ask how you escaped 'em. I'd never have looked twice at you!"

His grin faded a little. "You weren't afraid to bring a message to the East Side Slasher?"

"I've got to get back. It took forever to find the man who was supposed to give us the tour. See you."

He caught my wrist and held it in a firm but not painful grip. "Don't run off, Crissy. You don't believe all that crap, do you? You don't think I could have done what they say I've done?"

"No. I—don't know what to think."

"Terrific."

"I mean—no. I don't think you did what they claim you've done."

"Thanks."

I stared at him. He'd lightened his hair, for one thing. His hair and those incredibly thick eyebrows. He seemed to be all one color: beige—his hair, his eyebrows, his jacket, his pants. But his eyes were empty, dark brown and empty, like he had put *being* on hold until all this was over. Looking into those eyes even as briefly as I did was bewildering.

I didn't know what to say or think. I wanted everything to go back to being the way it had been: Gordon, the air-headed, pain-in-the-neck glamor boy. Nobody had to be his friend in those days. He had an endless tag-along of group-ies, and he had Francesca. He didn't need friends. He had his mirror, and he had Francesca.

He still had Francesca. Why did I suddenly have this urgent sense he needed *me* as well?

"I have to go, Gordon."

He smiled, a quiet little smile that was friendlier, warmer, realer than his big, devastating, for-the-balcony smile. "You really are Francesca's good friend, Crissy. She's lucky."

"Take care."

"Thanks a lot for coming."

"Sure." I started to go, and he stayed where he was. I turned my head in his general direction. "See you soon."

This time the smile was so devastating, I rushed away, slamming right into a tour group entering the American Wing. There were so many of them, I was bundled in among them for a minute, and I had to turn and spin and jerk around to work my way free. When I got to the big glass doors leading to the main route back to the rotunda, I looked around for Gordon. He had gone, retreated, vanished completely from sight.

When I got back to school and phoned my mother about Neva, she had already taken care of it.

"I remembered this morning," she admitted. "And I called Loretta right away." Neva's mom. "I was on my way out grocery shopping when you called. Tell Neva we'll have plenty of shrimp salad, brie, and French bread waiting for her. And I'll bake some brownies this afternoon. How late do you think rehearsals will be?"

"Nine, nine-thirty."

"You took money for cab fare, right?"

"Yes, Mom."

"Call when you're leaving school. In fact, I think I'll call Daddy's car service and have them pick you up."

"Mom—"

"I'm definitely going to do that, Cristina. Do you remember what they're called?"

"Vanguard."

"Vanguard. That's it. I'm going to call them right now. I'll tell them to be outside school at nine, okay?"

"That's a lot more expensive than a cab, Mom."

"Who knows how long it might take you to get a cab. You don't want those reporters to chase you around while you're trying to find one. I'll arrange for this from now through the run of the play. I don't know why I didn't think of it earlier. Drop off anyone you want on the way. There must be quite a few who live around here."

"Fine, Mom."

"Tell Neva we can't wait to see her."

I hung up and wondered why I felt so crummy. Then I remembered meeting Gordon and realized I'd wanted to tell my mother about it. If becoming a grown-up meant being sneaky and secretive, I wanted to slow down the process. Life was so much easier when I could tell Mom absolutely everything. We'd talk everything over, and when we were finished talking, all was right again with my little universe. I hated keeping stuff from her, but there was no way.

You really are Francesca's good friend. . . .

Everyone agrees Rob Emerson is the best actor among the boys in our company. Mrs. Halladay won't come right out and say that, of course, but she thinks so too. It's obvious the way she defers to him during auditions. And Shylock is absolutely the best piece of acting Rob's ever done. Mrs. Halladay's been hammering away at the rest of us, but Rob and I have done Act Four, Scene One exactly twice. In a Karen Halladay production that means you're good, don't worry about it. It's hard to believe this wizened, rasping, wretched creature just a few months ago was the bubble-brained hero in *The Boy Friend*, and before that O'Neill's emerging youth in *Ah, Wilderness!*

"My mom is Jewish," Rob told me when rehearsals started. "I wasn't even going to try out for this one, I was so sure she'd be—you know, hurt, offended. Shakespeare's pretty anti-Semitic. But Arandale"—Richie Arandale, another boy in Rob's class who does shows with us—"blabbed to her about it, and she practically ran me across town to audition. 'Shakespeare is Shakespeare,' she said. 'He wasn't

God, but nobody ever wrote a better play. And don't come home with any other part. I want to see you as Shylock.' She's something else."

I didn't see Francesca until we all showed up for play practice. By the time I got back from the museum, she'd gone on to another class. She grabbed me now and pulled me aside.

"Did you find him? Was he there?"

"He was, and I did, and I gave him your message."

She laughed, a short, nervous cough, really. "I knew he'd be there."

I stared at her. She hadn't known at all. She hadn't been sure for a single second that he'd be there.

She stared right back. "Well, tell me! What did he say? How do you think he looks?"

"I wouldn't have recognized him. He came up to me. Did you dye his hair?"

"Oh, Cristina, it's not *dyed*! I put some stuff on it to bring out the lighter highlights. It's the eyebrows that really make the difference. I did dye those."

"Whoa."

"You didn't know him, did you?" She was triumphant. "What did he say?"

"Not much. I was so late, I couldn't hang out with him."

"Hang out! My, my, we have softened, haven't we?"

"Don't be an idiot. I feel sorry for him."

"Do you? Odd. I had a strong sense you thought him guilty as charged."

"Me?"

She shrugged. "I'm delighted, of course. It's not very

151.

pleasant to have one's dearest friend despise one's *amour*."

"Come off it. Would I have carried your little message if I thought he'd actually . . . ?"

"You have a bad habit of not finishing sentences, Cristina. It's not worthy of you." And she sailed off to her crew waiting backstage, well aware I was ticked off and ready to throttle her.

Rehearsal seemed endless. Everyone's usually pretty cranky at the first late rehearsal, but even Mrs. Halladay was on edge. Nothing anybody did was good enough.

I had almost forgotten about the car service until I saw it waiting for us, right outside. I had forgotten to ask kids who lived near me to ride with us, but I was able to scoop up most of them as we left school. We had to run into the car to escape the flashbulbs popping all around us. It was like a bombardment of fireworks.

Stuffing eight teenage girls of varying weight and size into a car designed to comfortably seat five adults was a trip. The driver was a jolly gray-haired man with a nice smile and a lot of patience.

"I'm assuming one of you is Miss Garcia-Vasquez," he said.

"I am," I said. "Do you need to see ID?"

That made him laugh. "No, miss. That won't be necessary. I'm Frank. I'll be picking you all up for the next few weeks. And I didn't tell those newshounds who I was waiting for, neither."

"Thanks, Frank!"

"Now, if you'll tell me your addresses, one by one, I'll be happy to drive you young ladies to your doors."

"Thanks, Frank!" It was a chorus.

Each drop was a matter of a block to a block and a half. Ellie and Reenie and Marie-Lise were the first to be delivered, then Holly, Luisa, and Emily. Finally Neva and I were left to luxuriate in the roomy backseat. Frank remained jovial throughout.

"Where to now, miss?"

"We're together, Frank. Neva's coming home with me."

He nodded and turned onto an eastbound street.

"Thanks for being so patient, Frank."

"Pleasure, Miss Garcia-Vasquez, pleasure. I drive your dad a lot. Fine man. Gracious. Considerate. I appreciate that."

Neva was draping herself against the back of the plush seat like someone fantasizing about how it feels to be famous. She cracks me up.

"Excuse me, miss," Frank said. "I suppose those reporters were hot on your trail because of tonight's news."

I was afraid to ask. "What news?"

"That young man from around here who's suspected of killing that young woman."

"Gordon Larrimer?" I was choking on his name.

"Yes, miss. He failed to report in at the appointed time this afternoon. He's jumped bail, it seems. It was wrong to let him out so casual-like. Murder is a serious charge. The most serious charge."

Neva and I were gaping at each other in the darkness of the backseat, slivers of light from the street gliding across our faces as Frank slowed the car down to park in front of my building. Neva didn't know I'd met Gordon at the museum earlier. No one but Francesca knew.

And Gordon. Wherever he had run to.

I saw the police car the instant I stepped onto the curb in front of my building. It's no big deal; police cars are often parked on my street. It's pretty standard, in fact, for police cars to be parked almost anywhere at any time in New York City. For obvious reasons, this one made me nervous.

Neva noticed it too, but we didn't discuss it as we hurried into the elevator and rode up to my floor. When my front door was ajar, I knew I had a right to be freaking. Neva fell a step behind me as we went into the apartment, and there he was, the ferret-faced cop from the session at school. He was standing in our front hallway, and he was waiting for me.

My mother was right next to him, and she greeted us like he wasn't there. "Were you picked up? Was the car service there on time?"

I nodded twice, watching the policeman watch me. "Hi," I said to him.

"Hello, Cristina. You put in a long day for a high-school girl."

"I'm in a play."

"So I've been told. I'm sure you're very tired, so I'll try to make this as brief as I can."

"Why don't you go into the living room and sit down?"

My mother sounded a little frayed around the edges.

"Do you need me?" Neva hoped not.

Ferret-Face shook his head. "I'd like to speak to Cristina alone."

My mother wasn't so sure about that.

"It's okay, Mom." I wasn't so sure about that either. "Neva's probably starving."

"I'll bring you something." Mom eyeballed Ferret-Face. I'm Right Here, her eyes told him.

We went into the living room, he and I, and sat stiffly facing one another in front of the fireplace. I was desperate for a blazing fire. I was freezing, as though I'd been iced from the inside out.

"You've heard Gordon Larrimer has jumped bail."

"Yes. Just now. The driver told us."

"You saw him earlier today. You met with him at the Metropolitan Museum."

I felt weak, dizzy, sick. I must have looked guilty as sin.

"Do you deny that?"

I shook my head, the only communication I could manage. I wanted to ask him how he knew, but I guessed Gordon had been under surveillance. Some surveillance; he was gone.

My father was suddenly there, still in his overcoat, still clutching his briefcase. He glared hotly at the policeman, his face flushing bright red. "What's going on here?"

Ferret-Face stood. "Detective Lee Younger, Homicide Division. You are—?"

"Eduardo Garcia-Vasquez. This young lady's father."

"I have a few questions for your daughter, Mr. Garcia-Vasquez. She has just arrived home as well, and it is our understanding she was the last person to talk to Gordon Larrimer today."

My mother came in with a cup of something steaming hot on a tray, which she set in front of me. "Ed. I didn't hear you come in. This is—"

"I have just a few questions."

Daddy sat down heavily right next to me. He shrugged off his coat and let his briefcase slide to the floor. And never once did he take his eyes off Detective Younger, who pursed his lips sulkily before he sat back down himself.

Mom was quieter about it, but she sat nearby. I was sure Neva was pigging out in the kitchen.

"I don't know where he is, Detective Younger."

"How did you happen to meet him today at the museum?"

"I brought him a message from someone. I had to go to the museum on school business, and—I was asked to tell him something."

"What?"

"Excuse me, but how intense is this questioning apt to get?" My father was straining to stay calm. "Should I call my attorney?"

"That won't be necessary, Mr. Garcia-Vasquez. Your daughter is not suspected of anything."

"That's difficult to tell, sir. You're coming on very strong if information gathering is all you're doing here."

Younger eyed my father for a moment and then leaned toward me, cupping his hands together. "What message did you bring to Gordon Larrimer, Cristina? It might help us to know why he ran."

"We—my class, the junior class—were supposed to go to the museum on a field trip. My classmate told Gordon about it, so they planned to meet. Briefly. His mother does volunteer work at the museum."

"Yes, thank you, we know that. Please go on."

I glanced at my father, who took my hand and held it. "Our field trip was canceled, and my friend—"

"Who might that be, your friend?"

I looked at Daddy again, and he nodded. "Francesca Bernini-Winslow." I felt like The Informer. It really is a slimy, disgusting thing to rat on someone.

"What message did Francesca send?"

"She just wanted him to know she wouldn't be coming, she wouldn't be able to meet him."

"So," Younger rehashed it, "you were sent to notify the museum that your class would not be coming as scheduled. And Francesca, who was planning to slip away from the class—"

"Briefly," I insisted.

"Wouldn't her absence be noticed?"

I shrugged. "Sometimes you have to—excuse yourself. I'm sure she wasn't planning to be long." I wasn't sure of any such thing. I was trying frantically to remember whether Francesca had stayed for the entire rehearsal tonight. She hadn't left with us; I knew that for sure.

Detective Younger jotted some notes onto a small lined notepad he pulled from his breast pocket.

"That's homemade vegetable soup," my mother urged. "I put it in a mug so you can sip it easily. Go ahead. You must be famished."

I shook my head. I felt sort of sick, and tireder than I could remember ever being.

"You and Gordon Larrimer are pretty good friends," Detective Younger speculated.

"I've known him for a long time." Somehow that was stronger than I wanted it to be.

"And Francesca? She's a close friend of yours, right?"

"Yes." The closest. Why couldn't I say that?

"When did you last see her? Francesca?"

I stared at him. Had he read my mind or something? "She was at play rehearsal tonight."

"Does she have a big part in your play?"

"She doesn't have a part. She's the stage manager."

"Did she leave with you just now, get a ride, perhaps, in the car your mother sent for you?"

I shook my head.

"Do you know when she left school? Where she is now?"

"Home, I guess."

"Why wouldn't she come with you, get a ride with you? Your mother said you dropped off several people."

"She lives—closer to school. In a different direction from the rest of the kids who rode with me."

"Is that why you didn't take her? Perhaps someone else picked her up."

"I don't know. I didn't really see her when we were leaving school. There's always such a ruckus when we leave school. The press—"

"Was she there for the entire rehearsal?"

"I'm sure she was."

"Do you know for a fact she was?"

"Detective Younger," my father warned, leaning toward him. He gripped my hand so hard it hurt.

"A murder suspect is missing, Mr. Garcia-Vasquez." Younger spoke as if he were translating the information from another language.

"My daughter doesn't know where he is." Daddy left no doubt about that.

"Your daughter is the last person we know of who spoke with the suspect. If she can tell us anything—"

"She's told you everything she knows."

Younger sighed. "Please, Mr. Garcia-Vasquez, let me finish. I'll get right out of your hair if you let me finish. I have just one or two more questions for your daughter."

Daddy hesitated, then sat back, loosening his grip but not letting go of my hand. And he kept his eyes on Younger.

"Was Francesca there for the entire rehearsal? Did you see her as you were leaving?"

"No."

"She already told you that," Daddy objected.

"Would you like to telephone her?" Mom suggested quietly. "Please feel free to use our phone. Cristina can give you her number."

"Another detective has gone to her apartment."

"Then that should take care of it." Daddy pulled my hand up and kissed it lightly.

"Your daughter is still the last person known to have talked to Larrimer today. If Francesca hasn't actually seen or talked to him, your daughter is the strongest link we have for now."

The phone rang. Mom got up quickly to answer it. I wondered numbly whether it might be Francesca. She often called late like this.

"It's for you, Detective."

He crossed the room to take it. He was bigger than I'd remembered from that meeting in the junior lounge. That seemed such a long time ago.

Mom was hovering. "Try a little of that soup, Cristina. It's good. It really is."

"What a mess," Dad said.

"Francesca *would* ask you," Mom complained.

"I was the person Miss Delmar sent to the museum. Who else would she ask?"

"Too bad Miss Delmar didn't send Ellie. Why should she send you?"

"What difference does it make?" Daddy sputtered.

"Francesca wouldn't have asked Ellie."

"It's done," Dad said. "Cristina had a little lapse in judgment, but that's not a crime. She did what she did. What's the point of worrying what would have happened if someone else had been sent to the museum?"

Detective Younger was off the phone and heading for the front door. "Good night, folks. Sorry I disturbed you."

Daddy jumped up and followed him. "Have they found Larrimer?"

"No, sir." He pulled open the door.

"Does Francesca know where he is?"

Detective Younger took a step into the outer hallway and then turned back to Daddy. "We don't know where Francesca is." He turned "Francesca" into a sneer. "Her mother hasn't seen her since she left for school this morning."

If then, I knew.

"And she hasn't come home. She's gone too, it seems. Thanks for your cooperation."

Daddy closed the door quietly and applied all the locks we have to keep us secure. There are three, including a dead bolt.

We sort of stood around until Neva appeared from the kitchen on her way to my bedroom.

"Neva Williams!" Daddy greeted her, giving her a big hug. He has always been crazy about her, and it is very mutual. Neva's parents have been divorced for years. She never sees her father.

Daddy likes all my friends—everybody but Francesca. Where was she? Somehow I knew she was gone before the policeman said so. Had she had time to dye her hair and become as invisible as Gordon? I strained to remember when I'd seen her last. So much was always going on at rehearsal, and she was usually backstage well out of my sight. She could have slipped away at any time.

She might even be wearing a wig. Dyeing would take too long, even if she left rehearsal early. How had she contacted him? Why had they run?

Where were they?

"That soup is the best," Neva was telling me now.

"It's probably cold." My mother took the tray away.

"Don't fuss, Anne." My father was desperate to lighten things up. "Maybe Cristina doesn't like it scalding hot, the way you do."

"Francesca has gone," I told Neva, and I quickly filled her in on my stupid encounter with Gordon.

"Gone where? She was driving everybody nuts tonight." Neva was annoyed, remembering.

We all reacted together, practically pouncing on her.

"When did she leave?"

"Was she there the whole time?"

"Did she leave before we did?"

Neva looked from Daddy to Mom to me, folding her arms across her chest and taking her time deciding whose question to answer first.

"Neva—" I couldn't wait.

"Hold on, hold on! Maybe I should have been the one to deal with that cop."

"I wish you had." I did.

She smiled that sly little smile. "I'd have set his head spinning. He looks like something smells bad all the time."

"Tell us about Francesca," Mom persisted.

Neva thought about it. "She was really something tonight. The way she is just before we open. She raged around about the lights, the sound system, the set not being finished. And I think we're way ahead of where we usually are at this point. Anyway, she wouldn't let up. Everybody figured Mrs. Halladay had been on her case, but she was blowing everyone off. Whew!"

"Did she leave before we did?" I asked again.

Neva shook her head. "I don't remember. I was into it before we started doing Scene Two over and over and over again, but after that—"

"That was eightish." I wanted to pinpoint it.

"Later than that. I looked at the clock when we started it again for the forty-third take, and it was eight twenty-eight."

"That's eightish."

"There was a bulletin on during the Friday-night movie about Gordon's disappearance," Mom said. "Just before Detective Younger arrived."

"What time was that?" Daddy wanted to know.

"Nine. A little after nine. I thought it was you girls, ringing the doorbell, and I wondered why you didn't have your key,

Cristina. By the way, Neva, I have a key for you. Don't let me forget to give it to you."

"Let's see what the ten o'clock news has to say." Daddy hurried toward the den. Mom rushed after him.

"Did you have enough to eat?" she called back to Neva. "You'd feel better, Cristina, if you'd eat something."

I just stood there. I couldn't seem to move, and Neva, who was wandering along after my parents, came back to me.

"I don't want to watch the news," I moped. "I don't want to hear any more, know any more, think about it anymore."

"I hear you. You have had it." Neva looped her arm around mine.

"I have had it."

"I wouldn't mind lying down somewhere."

I had to smile, and we headed toward my bedroom. "I'm so glad you're here, Neva. I am losing it."

"You'll be fine," she said. "But you and Gordon have got to stop meeting like this."

I shot her a look and she cracked up, muffling it as we passed the den, where my parents were glued to the TV screen. She carried on right into my room, even after I closed the door.

"Okay, *okay*," I begged, collapsing onto my bed.

She sifted through my pile of CDs and found something she slipped into my disc player. The music of Annie Lennox filled the room, her bittersweet lyrics the perfect background for my darkening thoughts.

"Where'd she go, Neva?"

"With him, babe. It can't surprise you."

"But he's—This makes him a fugitive." That word, another word that has never meant anything to me before.

Another overheated word that has never had anything to do with my world. Just a word.

Like murder.

Or killer.

Or accomplice.

Gelber called me about an hour after Detective Younger left. Mom came to my room to tell me he was on the phone, and that was the first instant I remembered anything about our movie date. I had a flash of him waiting outside Cinema One with two tickets clutched in his hand, those beady little eyes squinting behind his glasses at the passing crowd, expecting the next person to step off a bus or out of a cab to be me.

"Ooops" was all I could think of to say when I picked up the receiver. I was too stressed out to be really upset about it, but I felt a twinge of guilt when I looked at the clock. It was almost eleven.

"You forgot," he said, and he sighed.

What had he thought I'd done? "I'm really sorry." I was, sort of. I hadn't done it deliberately.

"It's okay. I was able to sell your ticket."

He'd *sold* the ticket he bought for me?

"It's a good flick," he went on. "You'll have to see it sometime."

Flick. What a lame word. But I sensed he was about to

hang up and he sounded really bummed, which made me feel like a creep. "I'm really sorry, Alan."

"Yeah."

"Seriously!" Now what? "I have play practice tomorrow, but—" I could not believe I was doing this. "We're going to hang out, tomorrow night, probably go to Bouncer's, which can be really boring, of course. But if you'd like to come—"

Nothing for a few seconds, and then, "Yeah! Great! I'd love to."

I shut my eyes against it. But I'd screwed up and I owed him. It was also one way to handle things so my father would never find out. Before my life became so complicated, I usually went to Bouncer's on Saturday nights with the whole crowd.

"What time should I pick you up?"

"I'll meet you there. I absolutely promise, I will meet you there. At ten. You know where it is?"

"Sure."

"You go there all the time."

"I've never been there. But I know just where it is."

"Okay. See you tomorrow. Ten o'clock."

I didn't sleep very well. I decided around two-thirty that hunger might be my problem, so I went to the kitchen. I managed a few sips of that soup, which tasted really good, and a couple of Ritz crackers. My mother found me there. She never sleeps, or it seems that way to me. She's up before I am every morning, always up when I get home from a date, and if anybody's sick or can't sleep, she's around to hang out with them.

I was very glad to see her. There's something spooky about our apartment when there's nobody else around. She sat across from me at the kitchen table.

"I told you to eat something," she said, but she wasn't ragging on me; she was all sympathetic.

"We have rehearsal tomorrow," I reminded her, not having much else to say.

"I know. Neva's already told me what she wants for breakfast."

"You don't have to get our breakfast, Mom. I can fix Princess Neva whatever she wants. She certainly makes herself comfortable around here."

"I should hope so after all these years."

"Her mother spoils her."

Mom smiled. "Really. I'm glad she's so relaxed here. I love her."

"She's been asleep for hours. I wish I could sleep."

"Oh, Cristina! This is such an ordeal!"

My eyes filled suddenly and my throat tightened. "Where is she, Mom? Where'd she go? *Why?*"

She put her hand over mine. "I don't know, darling. Maybe he forced her to go with him."

That hadn't occurred to me. I rejected it. "He had me snowed. I saw him for two, three minutes maybe, and I didn't want to see him. I've always hated him. But when he turned the charm on yesterday, I melted like butter."

"Multiply that by a lot," Mom said. "Francesca's been under his spell for ages, and in a much more—intimate sense." It nearly killed her to say it. She kept hold of my hand and leaned closer. "Cris, do you think—could he actually have killed that girl?" She always cuts to the core of things.

"I don't know. I don't think so." I lowered my head and shook it, just once.

She tightened her grip on my hand. "Cristina, listen to me. Listen carefully. Nobody knows anything for sure, but you didn't think Gordon Larrimer was guilty yesterday, or you wouldn't have agreed to meet him at the museum. That's right, isn't it?"

I nodded.

"And he may not be guilty. He may be on the run because he's *not* guilty and doesn't know how to prove it."

"That actually sounds like Gordon."

"What I'm driving at is you haven't done anything wrong. Well, you shouldn't have agreed to meet him, but I'm sure it seemed harmless at the time. Francesca is so persuasive." She looked really pissed about that. She sat back and sighed, as if she were suddenly exhausted. She never let go of my hand, even though she had to stretch to hang on to it. "Learn from this, Crissy. There are always consequences. I'm sure you didn't want to meet Gordon."

"I didn't!" I sort of did, but if Francesca had nagged me, I'd have bailed, happily.

"Mrs. Billings is right: Janine is the forgotten victim in all this. It's as if the media is having a love affair with Francesca and Gordon, as though they're rock stars or something. It makes no sense, not a shred of sense." Something occurred to her, something really grim. "In a way, of course, perhaps it's best Janine doesn't interest them. She had such a tragic, lonely existence, and she made so many wrong choices. But she deserves to be mourned. No one should be savaged the way she was!" She patted my hand, signaling the end of our discussion. "They've done a very foolish thing, Francesca and Gordon. You're not to blame in any way for that."

Being up practically all night did not make getting up in the morning very joyous. I think I fell asleep—finally—about three minutes before Mom came in to call us. She put on quite a breakfast, and it was mostly her idea—Neva couldn't be that demanding—but I still left home feeling strung out, and it wasn't just the two cups of coffee. Being wired like this keeps your nerves jangling and your alarm system hot, so I was aware of the little black car from the instant we left my building.

I clued in Neva and she didn't turn around or argue with me or anything. She may have been humoring me, but she certainly knew better than to cross me.

When we were finally safely inside school, I peeked through one of the lobby windows. The press corps were settling in for as long as I'd be here, and sure enough, there was the little black car, double-parked across the street. I showed it to Neva.

"Cops," she said.

"You think?"

"Sure. Plainclothes, probably, but definitely cops."

"Why?"

"They're hoping you'll lead them to Romeo and Juliet."

I freaked. I looked around that lobby I'd been sailing through for twelve years like it might suddenly produce an escape hatch.

"Calm down," Neva advised softly. "Let's go lose ourselves to Willy the Shake. Come *on*."

She led me to rehearsal like I'd never make it on my own, and I looked up at the stage, already jammed with people, and prayed Francesca would be there. I didn't even notice when Neva slid over to talk to Mrs. Halladay. I became aware she wasn't right next to me, and by then she was waving at me to join them.

Rob Emerson came flying off the stage. " 'O noble judge! O excellent young man!' "

"Who are you calling 'young man'?" I was not feeling up to our usual banter.

"Whoops." He backed away, gesturing toward Neva and Mrs. Halladay. "You're being summoned."

When I reached them, Neva stepped nimbly aside and Mrs. Halladay pulled me up next to her. She's not into touching, so I was totally stunned.

"Neva's told me about the police questioning you last night, and the car following you this morning." She was murmuring in her most confidential manner. "Francesca's definitely run off with that boy, and she knew she was going to do it yesterday."

I waited to hear it all.

"She left pages with Ellie—*typed* pages—detailing the entire technical production. I've read it. It's brilliant. But it was not done in haste or at the last minute. She knew she would not be here to stage manage this production."

For the second time in twenty-four hours I was fighting having my eyes, nose, and throat fill up.

"Immerse yourself completely in this rehearsal," Mrs. Halladay urged. "Think of nothing but the play. Become Portia. You can do it, Cristina. Remember when you wanted to play Saint Joan?"

That was in eighth grade, lifetimes ago.

"I didn't think you could do it, remember? And you proved to me that you could. Unequivocally. Do that again. You need to."

She kept me very busy all morning. When she was staging a scene I wasn't in, she had me run lines with other people. Or check props. Or tag costumes. Or go over the music cues with Luisa.

Or go over the lighting cues with Ellie Blair. That gave me my first look at Francesca's masterpiece, the stage manager's script, complete, expert, carefully thought through step-by-step manual custom designed for this production. Mrs. Halladay had not overstated it. It was brilliant.

And it meant Francesca and Gordon had been planning The Great Escape for several days.

We rehearse from ten in the morning until three in the afternoon on Saturdays, and from noon until three on Sundays. On Saturdays, pizza is delivered to the school for the cast around twelve thirty. I got through the morning okay because I was so incredibly busy. But I nearly lost it during the lunch break. I kept thinking about Francesca and Gordon, about her actually planning all this ahead of time, about her going off with him to God knows where and putting herself in almost as much trouble as he was in.

She could be in danger as well. Mrs. Billings said Gordon was evil. *Evil* is an astoundingly strong word. My father says people don't believe in evil anymore because it's become so commonplace. They take it for granted, he says. It's everywhere.

"That makes it much more of a threat," Daddy says whenever he talks about it, which is every now and then when he thinks we need to hear it. I never really thought about it before—it was just one of Dad's diatribes—but it hit me now like a falling brick. "It looks like everything else. It's ordinary, and how can anything ordinary be fearsome?" He always pauses here. My father can be very dramatic when he feels the occasion demands it. "Beware," he finishes up. "Beware, when you look at something evil, and just because you have seen it before—often, perhaps—you turn away and say, 'Oh, that. Only that.' Beware. That will attack when you least expect it, use its poison to grip your insides, its tentacles to bind you outside, its power to overwhelm you. And you'll have no defense against it because you weren't alert, you weren't aware. Beware."

I was so bummed by the time we began to rehearse again, I could hardly remember my lines. I wasn't Portia. I was freaked-out Cristina, too tired to think or feel much of anything. Mrs. Halladay didn't let me stumble around for long. She decided to concentrate on the scenes I wasn't in and told me to help Markie assemble and label the props.

Markie seemed unaware of my deep despondency. She had her own problems. The ever-present Mr. Ender was drooping sleepily on his folding chair near the outer doors. The man doesn't read—not even a newspaper—and he doesn't wear a Walkman to listen to music or sports or the news. He just sits there, for hours and hours.

"I think your mother called my father," Markie chattered

away. She waited for me to react. "Are you listening to me, Cristina?"

"What did you say?"

"I think your mother called my father."

"Did she? What about?"

"Cristina! My father wants to send me away to boarding school."

"Oh, right. That's right. I forgot."

"You obviously told your mother before you forgot. I mean, she called my father, and I'm sure that's what it was about."

"I guess so, Markie. I'm sorry. I didn't sleep—What did she say to your father?"

"I don't know. I didn't listen in."

I knew she had.

"But he said he'd consider letting me stay on here. He said my going away might draw attention to me, especially if Gordon's trial gets the kind of publicity everybody thinks it will. He said he knows I'll be called to testify about the party, and he wouldn't want my being away at school to be taken the wrong way. I'm sure your mother started him thinking like that. He was so different about everything after he talked to her."

"I'm glad."

"She's amazing, your mother."

"She is."

"Frieda's working for Leslie Quinn's parents. Did you know that?"

"No, Markie."

"It seems Mrs. Quinn has been after her for years. I knew she wouldn't have any trouble getting another job." She hesitated, not a wise move since she was counting the plastic chips we use for ducats. "I miss her a lot, Cristina."

"I know, Markie. You can visit her at Leslie's."

"It's not the same. I always feel like I'm intruding, you know? She's glad to see me and all, but you know how rigid she is about getting her work done."

I didn't know. "Don't sweat it, Markie. I'm sure she's thrilled to see you anytime you go over there."

"It's not the same." Markie sulked, giving it up since obviously I didn't understand.

It was raining when we left school, sleeting really, and very cold. Brian was waiting for me in the lobby. He still had on his soccer uniform, and he was splattered all over with mud.

Seeing him was the only thing that actually penetrated my deep depression. When I realized I'd missed the Murray Hill game, I wanted to weep.

"Did you win?"

"Four to three." He was bursting with it. "I played. Coach Heibrun let me play."

"I can see that. How's your arm?"

"Okay."

"Brian?"

He waved me off with the other arm. "It's a little sore. It's bound to be a little sore. But we won!"

Neva was finally ready, and we set out for home. Everyone else had left long ago, but she had been closeted with Mrs. Halladay for what seemed like hours.

She is my understudy.

"You should have gone on ahead," she told us now, grimacing as the strings of sleet stung her face.

The weather had cut down the number of press corps ditzes following us home, but there were still a few diehards. And the little black car crawled along behind us as well. I felt like asking them for a ride.

"This is not going to be a night to go to Bouncer's," Neva said through clenched teeth.

"I'm not going anywhere," Brian announced. "I'm wiped."

I was kind of relieved about that. I hadn't figured out how I was going to explain Gelber to Brian, and I knew I could turn Neva around. All she needed was something to eat.

I was not prepared for what I found at home: my father raging around like a lunatic and my mother hiding in her room. She had obviously been crying.

"What happened?" I asked Alex. Neva had gone right to my room.

"Mom went Christmas shopping," Alex said, "and the paparazzi were so bad, she had to come home. They hounded her everywhere she went, and that drew crowds wondering what was going on, and that spooked the salespeople trying to wait on her. You know it must have been bad for her to cut and run home. It's all because of that TV show. I've never seen Mom so bummed. It stinks. The whole thing stinks."

"Dad's talking about moving," Mark piped up.

"What?" I didn't mean to, but I shrieked at Mark.

Alex shrugged. "Calm down. You know how Dad gets these offers every once in a while: to head up the office in London, Geneva, wherever. He says maybe we can't live in New York for a while. He's just crazed on account of Mom. You know he can't deal when she gets really upset."

I was glad to get out of there. Dad was off the wall when I said we were going out, but Mom called the car service and asked for Frank, and luckily he had another job in the area and could take us if we'd come home by one. I felt sort of like Cinderella, but it would give me a good excuse to duck out on Gelber.

I didn't have to look around for him. I mean, he was wearing a *suit*. It's a wonder they let him in, but there he was, in the gloom of the lobby entrance, watching the kids pour in, waiting for me. He didn't look stressed or anything. Actually, he looked sort of old.

He smiled that funny, crooked smile of his and came right over to us. Riding over, I'd told Neva about him, and for some reason she was psyched to meet him. Probably thought he could do something for her acting career.

"I got here early, before the line formed. And I paid your cover," he said. "I didn't know you were bringing someone. I'll pay for her as well."

"You don't have to do that," I said.

"Thanks a lot," Neva purred.

He paid, and we all went into the main room. Bouncer's used to be a movie theater, a million years ago when movie theaters were huge and showed only one movie at a time. The lobby at Bouncer's is enormous, and maybe when it was a movie theater and new, it was nice; but they keep it so pitch-black dark now, you have to wonder what they're hiding. The main room where everyone goes to dance used to be the theater part, but they took out the seats and now it's totally *black*. There are little white lights around the dance floor and leading the way everywhere. There's a stairway up to the balcony, where they have rooms for private parties. I've never been to one of those, but I have been invited. They can get pretty wild, I hear. Francesca goes to private parties at Bouncer's all the time, of course.

At least she did, before she took off with Gordon.

There are live bands at Bouncer's once a week. The other nights they have a great DJ, Rod Thornhill, "Thorny." I waved to him up in his glass-walled tower. All I could actually see were the glass walls, but he was in there. I knew that from the music blaring everywhere: Thorny's *sound*. There are TV monitors hanging from the ceiling that show music videos sometimes but now showed the dancers. Bouncer's is cavernous. Four or five thousand kids in there on a Saturday night is routine.

The bathrooms are where you never want to have to go. They're downstairs, and somebody's always really *sick* there. Vinyl sofas still line the walls in the area outside the bathrooms, leftovers from the old theater days when people hung out down there, waiting for the next show to start. Of course, they're ripped and grungy, a turnoff even in the dim light. I've only been down there once, and I'll never go again. Never.

The music was intense, and the floor jammed with undulating bodies. I love that word: *undulating*. It's so perfect for what we do to certain pieces of music, and it hit me I wouldn't be doing any of it tonight. Not unless I ditched Alan Gelber right here and now, and I owed him. I mean, I'm not into blowing people off. I sighed as Neva spotted some guy she knew and undulated onto the dance floor after him.

I looked around at Gelber. In the dark his glasses looked opaque, like sunglasses, shades. A nerd in a suit with shades; give me a break.

"Let's dance!" he said, moving onto the floor.

I hesitated—translation: didn't move a muscle—but I couldn't leave him out there alone, making a complete fool of himself, so I slid after him. When my eyes adjusted to the gloom, I glanced around to see who else was there. Leslie Quinn and that snooty Henry Lathrop were inching around each other like the wax figures they are. Can you imagine letting anyone call you *Henry*? Insisting on it? Luisa Pereira was right in the middle of the floor, moving as if every part of her anatomy had a separate—and running—motor. The girl can *undulate*! She always travels with the same guy: Hector somebody. He's from Chile too, and he's kind of cute, but I don't think it's anything really heavy. Ellie Blair was there with Rob Emerson, and they looked stunned when they saw me. I gave them my broadest How Long Has This Been Going On? grin. I wondered if Francesca knew about those two.

And that killed the moment, the music, my whole world. *Where was Francesca?* She was the Empress of this place. If she were here, she'd have a huge crowd around her.

"This is great!" Gelber was losing it out there, waving his arms, jumping around. He didn't need music; the man was spastic.

When Thorny finally put on something slow, I shouted

directly into Gelber's ear that I was dying of thirst, and he nodded and trailed me over to the bar that fills up the far corner of the main room. It was ten deep, but after I shouted directly into his ear what it was I wanted, he waded through the crowd and managed to come back in record time with beers for both of us. I inhaled mine. It was ninety-two degrees in there.

"You know everybody," he shouted directly into my ear as we watched the dancers. Swaying had replaced undulating; couples were basically holding one another up. A lot of people had bagged it and were standing around like us. One thing you can't do easily at Bouncer's is talk, but Gelber kept trying.

"You must come here all the time."

"Not really." Who could afford it?

"It's *great!*"

"It's okay."

"Hey, Crissy." Ellie Blair stepped out of the crush at the bar with Rob Emerson right behind her.

"Hey, guys. We should run a few lines, Shylock."

Ellie stared at Gelber as though he were neon or something. I introduced everyone.

The music picked up dramatically, and Ellie and Rob jumped back onto the floor together. They were really connecting. I had been further out of it than I'd realized not to have noticed.

Neva sailed by with two guys in tow. She flashed Gelber her million-dollar smile before launching into her special dance that is somewhere between impossible and illegal. Gelber was blown away by her. Those beady little eyes were burning holes through his thick lenses.

He wanted to dance again, but I stalled by asking for another beer, feeling only a passing twinge of guilt over it. Prices here are astronomical. He'd already paid out four times what the movie cost him, and I factored in the ticket he'd resold.

I led him out of the main room and into the lobby. There's a little more light out there because of the activity at the door. He kept looking around like there was something to see.

"I'm really sorry about last night." There wasn't anything else I could say.

He glanced at me. "Forget it. You should see the movie, though. It's not his best, but it's good." He went back to watching the practiced maneuvering of the man and woman managing the door. The man was a giant basically. We were supposed to think of a real bouncer when we looked at him, but he is actually a sweetie-pie. His name is Lars. He opened the door several times and let four or five couples in, but the crowd waiting on the street looked big. Some would wait an hour or more and still not get in. Why they keep trying is beyond me, but I've never had to wait more than fifteen minutes. Francesca was born on the A List, and I usually come to Bouncer's with her.

Where was she?

Gelber laughed. Or he might have coughed; it was tough to tell the difference. "Great," he murmured. "Absolutely great."

I hadn't a clue what he was carrying on about.

He insisted we dance again, and this time Neva manipulated him away from me, which was fine. He became hysterical: gyrating and throwing himself around. Other dancers had to clear a path for him or risk getting bumped or bopped. It was utterly mortifying.

I looked at my watch. Twelve-forty. Only twenty minutes more and Frank would be here to pick us up. And Gelber would turn back into the nerdy little snoop he really is.

When the time finally came, he couldn't believe there was actually a limo waiting for us.

"We could drop you," I offered weakly, praying he didn't live in Brooklyn or somewhere.

He shook his head. "Thanks anyway. I don't live anywhere near you."

Neva was still twinkling. "So nice meeting you, Alan."

Alan? "Thanks a lot," I mumbled, bummed it sounded so grumpy. But I *was* grumpy. I had been all night.

"I'd love to do this again sometime," he said.

Right.

"Super!" Neva bubbled.

"Why do I doubt we ever will?" He looked right at me.

Neva babbled all the way home, and I couldn't tell you what she said. I was looking for Francesca on every street corner.

The Merchant of Venice opened the Wednesday after our Thanksgiving break (which we spent most of rehearsing), ran for the customary five performances, with a matinee and evening performance on the final Saturday, and was, thanks to the TV and newspaper people, a fiasco. Crews from three local TV stations showed up on opening night and made a great mess out of things. We muddled through, but Mrs. Halladay went to Mrs. Whittaker and insisted the school hire beefy security people for all the other performances to keep out anyone not holding one of our unique, made-in-the-school-art-studio tickets. Unbelievable.

We got reviewed, for Pete's sake, like a Broadway show, in *New York* magazine. The review was nothing but a snide come-on for yet another article about Mom, *Weekend Closeup*, and the disgusting fallout from our segment, with a top layer of the latest dirt that could be dredged about the Billings murder.

My mother hasn't been out since the Christmas-shopping debacle except to see our play, the final performance. Even Mark got there, his very first outing and a tremendous personal high. Half his class were there because they had a brother or sister in our show, and they were much more excited about seeing him than the play, which they'd undoubtedly been dreading.

It sucks for Rob and Neva and all the other totally uninvolved people in the cast and crew who worked so hard and were so fabulous. The whole show has been blown up like some sort of grotesque floating balloon, much bigger than it was ever meant to be and utterly out of proportion. It's been made a feature, a colorful footnote of the Big Story, the horror show that started at Markie's party with that broken beer bottle.

I can't believe any of it, yet there's no room in my life for anything else. I don't go anywhere anymore; none of us do. Brian and Alex and Mark and I are reaching the highest levels on our computer games. We play them endlessly. My mother's ordered all her Christmas gifts by telephone, and she's finished writing her Christmas cards, a first. Christmas cards from my mother usually arrive around mid-February. Nobody cares, because she writes great, long, funny catch-up notes on each one, and lots of her friends save them and talk about putting them together in a book. That was before all this started, of course. It used to be a joke. It would probably make the best-seller list after all this nonsense.

I've been thinking a lot about Janine Billings lately. And I dream a lot, something I never used to do. My dreams are mixed up, exhausting, hard to explain, and scary. Janine's in a lot of them. I'm not sure I'd remember what she actually looked like if her mother hadn't written that letter. Her yearbook picture that's been used so much looks plastic, totally fake. But her mother's description haunts me:

> *Janine was not a pretty child. . . . She had a plain little face, stick-straight, flyaway hair. . . . She bit her fingernails and wound one strand of hair so incessantly, it stuck out from her head no matter what she slicked onto it to keep it down.*

I see that girl in my dreams, winding that strand of hair around one finger, winding and winding. And waiting. For what? I'd never know, because I never said a word to her. How many other people will walk through my life without my seeing them?

I dream about Francesca too, so I guess that means I'm

really worried about her, even obsessing over her disappearance. Francesca and Gordon have been missing without a trace for over three weeks. I get pissed sometimes. I wonder whether she's off somewhere with him, laughing at all the coverage in the newspapers and completely uncaring about the anguish she's causing. Maybe even proud of it.

When I came home from school at noontime on the day we finally got out for Christmas break, I nearly lost it when I went into our living room and found my mother with Mrs. Bernini-Winslow. My first wild flash was that Francesca was dead. I'd had one of my dreams the night before, and she'd been in it, and there'd been a lot of running around and getting nowhere and a strong sense of danger, for her and for me. I'd been wiped out all day from it.

I must have just stood there and stared, because my mother finally gave me one of her fixed What's Wrong With You? smiles and said, "Why don't you join us, Cristina? I'm sure you're as delighted to see Mrs. Bernini-Winslow as I am."

I dropped my backpack, which weighed even more than usual since I'd had to clean out my locker entirely that day. They always paint and scrub and try to restore the school building while we dear little destroyers are on vacation.

Francesca's mother is not exactly beautiful, but she is so elegant, so supremely chic and perfectly turned out, she overwhelms any room she is in. She knows this and takes it completely in stride. Francesca's disappearance hadn't affected that one bit, as far as I could tell.

"How are you, Cristina?" She has a lovely voice and very clipped, precise diction, which makes her sound too cultured to be an American, especially a New Yorker, which is exactly what she is.

"Fine, thank you, Mrs. Bernini-Winslow. How are you?"

She smiled rather sadly and looked at my mother.

"Mrs. Bernini-Winslow is nearly frantic, Cristina," my mother spelled it out for me. "Naturally."

She didn't look frantic. I couldn't imagine her looking remotely frantic. Ever. And certainly not over Francesca.

"She hasn't tried to contact you, Cristina?"

"No, Mrs. Bernini-Winslow." I wish.

"You'd tell me, wouldn't you? You can imagine how it is for me, not knowing—anything."

My long-standing resentment began to weaken. Maybe she meant it. Maybe she *was* worried.

She stayed for only a few more minutes. When she stood to go, Mom and I got up, like two robots preprogrammed to move when she did. I walked a few steps behind them to our front door.

"I shouldn't have just dropped in like this," Mrs. Bernini-Winslow said.

"Of course you should have," Mom forgave her. "We're all so distressed. We're all terribly worried."

"It's so very helpful to know that."

Why were they saying everything but what mattered to them? I trailed Mom to the kitchen.

"I will never get over *that*," she said. "When I think of the times I've invited her here: to tea, to dinner, for those Parents' Association lunches. I even asked her to a bridge party once. I don't think she even acknowledged it."

"I nearly passed out when I saw her."

"She's desperate," Mom deduced. "She's at the absolute end of it."

That was the first time I ever wondered whether it was Francesca or Francesca's mother my mother disliked.

I have slept through the first four days of Christmas break. I miss having Neva around. She was with us for over a month, and her mother came for Thanksgiving and stayed in the guest room for several days afterward, which was fun. But it really is easier without them.

It's like we're under quarantine or something. Dad still goes to his office every day, but nobody else leaves the apartment. People come here, especially Mark's friends, and Mom has the groceries and everything else delivered. Dad picked out an enormous tree, as he does every year, had it sent right home, and Mom decorated it immediately. We usually stash it in our back hall until Christmas Eve and do everything then. By the time Christmas actually arrives, we'll feel like it's already happened. And Mom's hyper this year about Keeping Spirits Up. I just hide in my room, play my stereo, smoke a lot, read a little, and sleep. I could grow old this way.

Mom listens to every newscast on the radio and watches the TV news incessantly. I watch only my soaps and VCR movies. Alex gets a lot of mail from Yale, and that's the big high for everyone. Plus Brian's over a lot, to see me as well as Alex. I think I'm becoming unbelievably boring to be around, but I must be okay in a clinch because we have a lot of those when he's here.

The case hasn't made the front pages for a while, but I

guess we'll be fodder for the paparazzi until the whole thing is somehow resolved—with Gordon's trial for murder (if they ever find him), or someone else stepping up to admit they did it (likely!), or some disclosure that will give a final, incontestable answer to the million questions that keep piling up.

I don't really mind staying in, which is weird. Mom keeps me busy (when I'm awake) with a lot of chores and stuff. Every closet in this apartment has been completely over-hauled and reorganized. No wonder Fischer misses her. The woman should run the world, she's so orderly. I may get fat, I'm eating so much, but I can't worry about that right now. Everything comes under the heading of Therapy at the moment: sleep, videos, staggering amounts of self-indulgence. It's probably all very addictive.

Alex is teaching me how to play bridge. Dad taught him years ago, and they've played in a couple of tournaments together. It seems like a fun thing for the four of us to do when Mark's gone to sleep. Mom's a good player, though not in Daddy's league, and when her chin goes up, you know she's got a good hand.

Alex dealt out the cards one dark afternoon when it had begun to snow and Brian called to say he couldn't come over because his mother needed him to go shopping with her. Mom was locked in her room organizing and wrapping a pile of presents that had just been delivered that morning, and Mark was asleep. I had made some penuche fudge, and I think Alex was so shocked at my blatant hedonism, he was using the bridge lesson to turn my head (and appetite) to things more intellectual.

"Okay," he said after dealing out four hands, displaying

two opposite each of us and arranging his own. "We'll do it this way: I'll be the theoretical closed hand, and you play the contract. I've arranged the cards accordingly. I'm the dealer, so I open the bidding and—pass."

We were still at it an hour and a half later when Dad came in, soaked from the snow, carrying a fistful of mail. It now takes our doormen all day to sort the holiday load. My father is obsessive about mail. It's definitely because he handles so much paperwork in his job, but he goes through it like lightning, hands out what's not his, and then hounds everybody to get rid of anything nonessential. We're so used to him, we don't pay much attention unless someone who's never seen it before is around.

"This is for you," he said now, handing me a pile. He put it right on top of my little stash of taken tricks, which annoyed me. He handed Alex his mail. "Where's your mother?"

"In your room," I said. "Knock first. She's wrapping."

He gave me an Are You Serious? look and headed down the hall. I glanced at my mail. Right on top was a soggy postcard from Bouncer's inviting me (and the hundred others on their A List) to a "holiday party." I saw that Alex had gotten one as well.

"Want to go?" I teased. "We could lend an air of notoriety to the whole scene."

"I wouldn't darken the door of that place," he growled. "Kate and I went there once with some friends of hers, and we left after fifteen minutes. Everybody in there was stoned."

"Don't exaggerate." Something tugged at my memory, something beyond that bogus night with Neva and Alan Gelber. "You go to the movies around there."

"What are you talking about?"

"You saw Francesca and Gordon coming out of Bouncer's, the night of Markie's party. She told me. She said you were coming from Cinema One."

He remembered. "Yeah. But we only saw Francesca."

I regretted bringing it up. "She was with Gordon."

"No, she was by herself, hailing a cab. I offered to take her home with us, but she said something about meeting Gordon uptown. Then a cab came and she took off. We came home on the bus."

I couldn't say anything. Truthful Alex with his total recall. He had seen only Francesca, because Gordon wasn't with her. He was somewhere else.

The snow Dad had struggled through to get home that night turned into rain, and our prospects for a white Christmas were dim. It didn't matter. We certainly weren't going anywhere. But it made looking out the window a real downer. Everything was *gray*, like an underexposed black-and-white photograph. Gray.

Alex has begun to go out again. He was like some kind of caged animal after a week of staying in. He nearly wrecked Dad's total gym, which is kept in the back pantry with the washer and dryer.

"I'm going to run around the reservoir," Alex told Mom.

"If those media people are out there, they'll have to catch me to talk to me."

I wanted to remind him to be back for my bridge lesson, but I suspected that once he got a taste of freedom, he'd stay out there.

"Don't get cold," was all my mother said. "You'll work up a sweat, running, so don't hang around in wet clothes."

I waited for her to say We Don't Want to Have Anyone Sick for Christmas, but she didn't. Was she bagging Christmas? Maybe it just wouldn't happen this year.

I think I'm spending too much time by myself.

We still let the answering machine take all our calls. The phone calls and heavy mail seem to run according to the press coverage of the Billings story, especially Francesca and Gordon's disappearance. When there's a big story about it, or a run of pictures—or, as had just appeared, a profile of Francesca and her glamorous parents (the article was totally definite about the English movie director being her father)—we get a lot of mail and phone calls. We don't even have to know about the new publicity to *know* about it. Besides the regular Christmas stuff, Mom averages sixty pieces of mail in a day; our mailman must love us!

Laney Conlon and a couple of boys from Mark's class arrived to hang out with him just after Alex went for his run. Mom was in the den answering her mountain of mail and asked me to monitor the calls. I set up the answering machine in my room so I could listen to my stereo. I've discovered classical music during my hibernation. My punk-rock sounds were making me sort of crazy, and Mom suggested I listen to some stuff she finds "soothing." I didn't take her up on it right away, naturally, but I finally got around to listening to some Mozart a couple of days ago, and I've been OD'ing on it ever since. It's really cool. It's hard to fathom all this stuff being written before synthesizers. I mean, a lot of it is incredibly dimensional.

I was listening to piano music—Andre Watts playing a funky prelude by George Gershwin, of all people—when the phone rang. I almost answered it. Maybe it was a slow news day; it hadn't rung for hours. I was so into the music, I almost forgot about the answering machine and answered the old-fashioned way.

"You have reached . . ." the message tape droned. Alex was the Voice for this week. We change it all the time, but I had to smile, listening to him be Official.

When the message was finally over and the pesky beep sounded, someone hissed, "Shit!" and then there was a long pause before whoever it was spoke again.

"This is *Seventeen* magazine calling," a woman finally said. She had a kind of singsong voice, very nasal, the way you'd sound if you'd been delivering the same message over and over for days. "We're calling to verify your address, since we have a gift subscription for Miss Cristina Garcia-Vasquez—"

A perfect pronunciation of my surname, which never happens . . . and something about the perfect pronunciation . . . I was half listening after *Seventeen* was mentioned. I considered myself too old for *Seventeen* when I was twelve. Who would be dense enough to think I'd want a subscription?

I sat up so fast I almost stopped breathing. I clicked off the answering machine and picked up the phone. "Hello? *Hello?*" I knew who this was. What I didn't know was whether she'd actually speak to me.

"Did you stop the tape?" Francesca asked me, half in and half out of her pretend voice.

"Where are you?"

"Did you—?"

"*Yes!* Where are you?" I repeated, forgetting all about the caller-ID box.

"I'm nearby," Francesca said.

"Are you home?"

"No."

"Francesca—where are you?"

"You'll call out the troops."

"I won't!" I wanted to. "Francesca—"

"Promise you won't tell a soul."

"Why?"

A pause. "I'm going to hang up, Cris."

"Don't hang up!" She didn't say anything, but I didn't hear a click, so I gripped the receiver and waited.

"Promise," she insisted very quietly.

"I promise." I had to.

"I'm at Aunt Winnie's."

For an instant I thought she was playing one of her weird, cruel jokes, but then I remembered Aunt Winnie. She was Francesca's favorite relative. She was actually her great-great-aunt. She used to live on Cornelia Street. She was an old lady when we were little, so she'd be ancient by now.

"Cris, are you still there?"

"I'm here. I thought Aunt Winnie had moved to Florida."

"She did, but she kept her house. I've always had a key, as you know."

I didn't know. I'd never known.

"We probably won't be here much longer."

We. "Where are you going?"

"I'm not sure."

"You've been there—at Aunt Winnie's—all this time?"

"Most of it."

"Francesca—"

"I miss you, Crissy. What's new?"

"What's *new*?"

"I'm sure the show was wonderful."

"Francesca, Gordon's got to turn himself in. You're in as much trouble as he is, almost."

"He didn't do it, Cris. Nicky did, and he blamed Gordon to save himself. We've got to help him. He'll never get a fair trial in New York."

"He's not helping himself, jumping bail like this."

"You don't understand. I didn't, at first." She stopped abruptly. When she went on, her voice was different, quieter and fiercely intense. "Could you bring me some money, Cris? I'll pay you back. Every cent. We're going to fly to California to see my father. He'll help us. I know he'll help us."

It was the first time in our entire friendship she had ever mentioned her father. "How d'you know?"

"I called him. I took a wild chance and called him. I haven't talked to him in *years*." Another pause. She was whispering now. "He was wonderful. He told me to come; he said he'd do whatever he could."

"But what can he—?"

"People can do things, Cris! People like my father have marvelous connections. I have some money, but not enough to get us both to California. I need about two hundred."

"Two hundred!"

"You have it," she challenged me. "You know you do. You

make all that money every summer and stash it in that fat savings account of yours."

And need it all, for my spending money. To her, two hundred was like twenty, but we were talking about the bulk of my dwindling bank account, and she'd never pay it back.

"I'm counting on you," she rasped. She hung up.

The first time I visited the house on Cornelia Street, Francesca and I were in seventh grade. I was twelve, she was about to be, and we knew absolutely everything. Well, she did, and she told me all about it.

There was a little shop on the street level, Aunt Winnie's long-time tenants. They sold odd bits of jewelry made of silver with jade and onyx, and the place was so jam-packed with display cases and weird pieces of statuary, it was tough to move around. I always felt bulky and incredibly clumsy there, and I never went in or out without knocking something over. The two old men who ran the place were nice enough. You could tell they thought Francesca and I shouldn't be wandering around Greenwich Village alone. My parents would have agreed. This was when I began to hone my "fudging" skills.

The smaller, thinner man was always pleasant. Aunt Winnie said they had lived together for thirty years or more, which prompted Francesca to explain homosexuality to me. In detail. I didn't fully get it until a couple of years later, when I realized how thoroughly she grasped her subject. That sort of thing definitely came under the heading of Reference, for Francesca, and therefore had to be dealt with accurately and without any frills or fudging.

Aunt Winnie lived on the top three floors, up a rickety set

of uncarpeted (and, I always suspected, unsafe) wooden stairs. On the first floor (which was really the second floor, above the jewelry shop) she had her studio, where she worked for several hours every day. We always came to visit in the afternoon, because she used the morning light for her painting and wouldn't answer the telephone or doorbell while she was working.

On the next floor were her bedroom, a small kitchen, her sitting room, and the bath. I never went beyond this, but Francesca said there were two small bedrooms and another bath on the top floor. She had walls lined with bookcases and an out-of-tune Steinway grand piano as the centerpiece in the sparsely furnished sitting room. I vaguely remember studio couches lining the walls where there weren't book-cases, and everything had a musty, unkempt look. House-keeping didn't interest Aunt Winnie in the slightest, but Francesca loved to list her possessions like a tour guide in a museum. She had a sculpture by Frederick Remington, a Turner ("from his yellow period," Francesca would always say), framed sketches and drawings, a massive oil by her brother (Francesca's great-grandfather, the oddball who made it into the Modern Museum) over the fireplace, and a large assortment of the most astounding photographs I have ever seen. Many of the top photographers working then were her close friends, and there was a portrait of her, a black-and-white photograph by some big name who worked a lot for *Life* and *Vogue*, that is the single most unforgettable picture I have ever seen. She looked so young in this shot; I knew her only as a wizened, rather stooped and shrunken old lady with so many deep lines in her face, she looked accordion-pleated—and it was a tight closeup of her, laughing. I had to laugh, looking at it; everyone did. Aunt Winnie laughed easily and often. She was sharp and sarcastic, and I know a lot of Francesca's best one-liners were hers originally. In fact, Francesca's whole style of speaking and the way she sees things is so much like Aunt Winnie's, it's spooky. It may have to do with genes and inherited personality traits, but Francesca adores Aunt Winnie. She was devastated when she moved to Florida.

"She's keeping the house," she *had* told me, a year or so ago, when Winnie finally left New York for good. "The shop's become a boutiquey sort of place, full of pricey potpourri and fancy soaps and all that. The little silversmith died, and his widower retired to the Caribbean or somewhere. Aunt Winnie says she'll keep the house until she's too dotty to cope, or dead altogether, and then it'll come to me in her will. She says as long as she can say, 'I have a house in New York,' she'll feel she hasn't completely let go of life the way she likes to live it."

I didn't know why I hadn't thought of Aunt Winnie's house before. It seemed so obvious now. It was incredible the police hadn't found them there. Why wouldn't Francesca's mother have looked there?

Then I remembered Francesca's mother hadn't gotten along with Aunt Winnie. At all. Aunt Winnie called her "spoiled" and "shallow." She told Francesca once when I was there: "You have great flair. Don't let it become the sort of arch phoniness your mother affects. I think you're actually much, much brighter than she ever was."

But why had she taken Gordon there? It made me furious to think she'd involved Aunt Winnie in this scummy business. Wait 'til the press corps got wind of it. They'd crawl all over the house on Cornelia Street and write it up as a "safe house," as though crack dealers hung out there.

The press corps. How was I going to get anywhere near Cornelia Street without becoming a human arrow pointing directly to Francesca and Gordon?

I almost bagged it. I thought about calling Francesca back, telling her I was really sorry, but. Why wouldn't her mother's contacts be just as powerful as her father's? It would be so easy to do the right thing: Tell Mom, who'd call Mrs. Bernini-Winslow, who'd call the police.

I couldn't do that. It went against every instinct, but somehow I knew I had to go. I had to do what Francesca had asked me to do, and somehow avoid exposing them and myself.

I told Mom I was going Christmas shopping. She was half asleep after a long soak, stretched out on her chaise in a plaid bathrobe I hadn't seen in a while. I hoped she thought I was just getting antsy, like Alex.

"Pick up some extra gift tags, will you? We never seem to have enough."

"What'll I wear?" I waited for her antenna to go up. "I don't want the Peeping Press making a scene everywhere I go."

One eyebrow raised, but only slightly. She knew better than anyone that I wasn't exaggerating in the least. She pulled herself off the chaise, rooted around in her closet, newly organized and pristine, and piled "possibilities" on her bed: a blond, braided wig she'd worn in the Parents' Association show when I was in sixth grade; a big brown felt hat with a scarf attached that covered the ears and tied around the chin; a lavender quilted coat she'd bought when everyone was buying them that she'd always hated. I thought she'd given it away, it had been so long since she'd worn it. I tried everything on, but we had to bag the wig, it was so bulky under the hat; and the hat covered so much, I didn't need the wig. I looked like something out of a road company cast of *The Sound of Music* in it, and anyway, it made my head itch.

She found a pair of old eyeglass frames in the top drawer of her bureau. They were tortoiseshell and quite thick, but she stuck her fingers through and wiggled them to show me there were no actual lenses. "Don't ask me where these came from; your grandmother probably. She never throws anything away, but somehow I always end up with things." She shook her head. "Don't ask."

I looked like an utter dork. I mean, those frames changed my whole face. I could probably have worn the glasses and my own clothes and pulled the whole thing off. There was no convincing my mother of that, however.

I was finally ready. I felt like I was wearing a sleeping bag, that quilted coat was so puffy and suffocatingly warm. Mom cracked up, but she kept it under control because she knew I was ready to rip everything off. What she didn't know was how incredibly motivated I was to be *invisible*.

What she didn't know was where I was actually going or why.

Jerry the doorman didn't know me. He gave me a long, hard

stare as I sailed out of the building. There was a mild flutter among the press corps that made my heart stop, but I kept on going toward Lexington Avenue, and they didn't. I couldn't believe it until I was on the subway and headed downtown. I was out of my apartment, and no one was following me!

I nearly died of the heat on the train. The glasses kept slipping down my nose, and I had to open that lavender cocoon I was stuffed into. I was dying to take off the hat, but I didn't dare. I tried very hard not to look at anyone. I read an ad in Spanish for prenatal care about three hundred times, wishing I'd brought a paperback to pass the time, knowing I was too wired to read anything.

I couldn't seem to calm down. I was hyper, freaked out, so close to the edge I probably would have screamed if anyone had spoken to me for any reason. I tried to think things through, to anticipate what I might find at Aunt Winnie's, but my mind was on overload. I'm sure my pulse was racing. I was a jangling mass of raw nerve endings wrapped in a massive quilt with a "lid" of dark-brown felt I was sure I could blow off at will.

The train was crowded with a lot of tired-looking people, many lugging holiday shopping bags. It was too early in the afternoon to be completely packed with business commuters. These people were shoppers, some working people keeping earlier hours, a few kids my age hanging out together, out of school for the holidays with too much time and no cool way to spend it. It's hard to figure out everybody on a subway car. The regulars are easy. Their eyes have a Will This Ride Ever End? look.

I got out at Bleecker Street. There was a bank cash machine right nearby where I could withdraw the money she'd asked for. I wasn't going directly to Cornelia anyway. I wanted to be sure no one was tailing me, not press, not police. I got my cash, then wandered across Bleecker on to Sixth Avenue, went into a little card store and bought the gift tags Mom wanted, in case I got rattled later and forgot them. The coat had enormous pockets, so I had my wallet and house keys stuffed into one, and now I pushed the little bag with the gift tags into the other. Nobody gave me a second look. I felt like a mattress walking around. And that hat!

I love the Village. It is my favorite part of my favorite city. It has everything, and everybody does his own thing with complete abandon. Nobody looks, nobody cares. The only thing that doesn't fly in the Village are fur coats. Mom wore hers once when we were all going to a play at the Public and some guy handed her a printed card that said, "The original owner of that coat was brutally murdered so that you could wear it." She was bummed out for the rest of the evening.

I go to the Village whenever I get the chance. Obviously I hadn't been in quite a while. But there was something very strange about being there now. I was one step ahead of a fit, things kept going in and out of focus, but finally I headed for Cornelia. If anyone was following, he'd fooled me. I kept turning every which way, trying to spot a tail. Swiveling around like that, tied into that hat and wearing eyeglass frames that slipped, wasn't easy. I felt like a reject from some far-out Halloween party. There was more trick than treat involved in this little caper.

Number 5. Aunt Winnie's house was Number 5. The street-level shop was unrecognizable. The security grate was down, and peering through it revealed a hand-printed sign pasted on the shop window. "Happy holidays. Back January 6." A small display of hand soaps and bags of potpourri looked sad and sort of trivial, and I felt a twinge for the old silversmith. I wondered what had happened to all the display cases and those pre-Columbian voodoo dolls or whatever they were.

I was stalling, letting my mind wander. I could still split, go home, tell Mom the truth, no harm done.

Wimp. Scaredy-cat. Lily liver. Call yourself a friend. She needs you. Francesca needs *you.*

I finally looked up at the big studio window, half expecting Francesca and Gordon to be standing there, looking down at me and laughing their heads off. But there was no one, nothing. I remembered we could always see one of Winnie's big abstract paintings from down here. We could see it clearly, hanging on the wall, from exactly where I was standing now, on the sidewalk. But there was no painting, nothing visible; only a blank expanse of wall. It gave me a queer feeling. If Aunt Winnie's old rooms were empty, where was Francesca?

I finally couldn't stand it. I'd gotten this far. Do it! I climbed the outside stone steps and reached the front door. Now what? Ring the bell? Have someone come on the intercom and tell them, "I've come for Francesca. I've brought the money she asked for."

I didn't ring the bell. I tried the front door and it was open. I stepped inside after another swivel view of the street. Cornelia Street doesn't draw the crowds of, say, Bleecker or Christopher. The tourists march up and down West Eighth or Waverly or University. Older people like to walk along the edge of Washington Square Park and look at the old town houses and talk about Henry James. One of my former English teachers told us that.

My mind was like a video on fast forward, running wildly out of control. I forced myself to adjust to the lack of light in that little hallway, and I focused on the stairs, facing me like a dare. Come on. You know the way. You've climbed me lots of times.

It was frigid. Even packed into my bunting, I could feel it. Damp, dusty, long-term. When had the shop downstairs closed for the holidays? A week ago? Longer? If the place was empty and the heat turned off, how could Francesca and Gordon be here? If the heat was off, the electricity was probably off as well, and it was getting dark quickly.

I headed up the stairs in a spurt. They still squeaked and buckled with every step. If I'd stepped right through any one of them, it wouldn't have surprised me. I hurried, and the climb was steeper than I'd remembered. I'd never been nervous making this climb before. Going to Aunt Winnie's had always been a trip, the most fun, a great adventure.

I got to the second floor and walked into the studio. It was utterly bare: no easel, no stacks of canvases, no strong smell of paint and turpentine, no drop cloths, no model's platform, nothing. Well, maybe she was still painting. In Florida. She probably was still painting, knowing Aunt Winnie. She'd keep painting 'til she dropped.

I ran up the next flight and rushed into the sitting room. I gasped at the stark, shadowy emptiness I found there. No Steinway, no studio couches, no photographs or paintings, no Turner in his yellow period. Nothing but stained, empty walls with brighter spaces where the treasures had hung.

I looked down the staircase. It was rapidly becoming a very black hole as the last of the daylight faded. I should go home. *Go home.*

I looked up the final flight. I had never been up there. I was not going up there now. Just ahead of me was the oddly shaped little bathroom with its funny porcelain tub with the carved cat's paws, four of them, holding it up off the cracked tile floor. There was a metal ring overhead for the shower curtain, an afterthought and obviously so, a homely convenience blaring the fact that Aunt Winnie couldn't have cared less about practical things as long as they worked.

I finally had to take a step or two toward the bedroom. Aunt Winnie's bedroom. Francesca had showed it to me once, on the sly. We'd laughed at its clutter, the unmade bed, the pile of dirty laundry in one corner. The old girl was as slobby as we were, without maids or Mom to pick up after her. I remembered feeling sort of creepy, like we shouldn't have been in there, like we were betraying all the goodwill and fun talk and warm welcome Aunt Winnie had always extended us.

It'll be empty, like the rest of this place. There's nothing here, no one here.

But there was someone, just beyond the door that stood ajar, facing me. I froze to the spot where I stood, knowing someone else was there.

Waiting.

"Francesca?" I kept looking down the stairs, ready to pitch myself down them in half the time it had taken me to get up there.

"Crissy!" She came flying out from behind the bedroom door, Gordon looming behind her like a hulking shadow. She nearly knocked me down, throwing her arms around me. It had to be like hugging a huge pillow. "Oh, Crissy! I knew you'd come! Didn't I tell you she'd come?"

Gordon nodded. He was smiling, I think. He looked sort of sleepy, like my arrival had wakened him. He leaned over and kissed my cheek lightly. We could have been meeting at a cocktail party or Bouncer's or somewhere, things were so terribly cordial. They were both wearing overcoats, tightly and completely buttoned.

"I didn't think anyone was here. It's freezing."

"The people who run the shop downstairs went on vacation four days ago and turned off the heat," Francesca said. "We don't have access to the boiler room. But you get used to it. Well, you have to keep bundled up. . . . You look hysterical. Where'd you get all that stuff?"

"My mother put it together."

"Your mother?"

"She thinks I'm Christmas shopping. It's a long story. Relax. She doesn't have a clue where I am or why."

"I've never been so glad to see anyone in my life! Come

on in." She led the way into the bedroom, which was much less cluttered than I remembered but had a few pieces of furniture left in it, including Aunt Winnie's big old mahogany four-poster bed, which took up most of the space. It was piled high with coverings, including what looked like a tapestry or a rug on top. I was sure that was where Francesca and Gordon had been spending most of their time in this frigid place. Somehow, realizing that was a major turnoff.

"Have a drink," Gordon offered, lifting a Scotch bottle from a little round table with a long, fringed cover. "We're into insulation around here, big time."

"No, thanks. Francesca, I brought your money."

"You are a dream, Crissy! I will pay back every cent, with interest. I couldn't use my credit card. I'm sure the police are just waiting for me to do something like that."

"I can't believe they haven't found you here."

"Dumb luck, with the emphasis on the dumb."

"Why wouldn't your mother think of this place?"

"My mother?" It was a sneer. "My mother's only been here twice in her whole life, about a million years ago. Aunt Winnie didn't exist for my mother, and the feeling was very mutual."

"Was your father surprised to hear where you were?"

Francesca looked blank.

"Your father?" Gordon slurred.

"You didn't tell him where you were."

"You talked to your father?" Gordon shook his head.

"You didn't talk to your father," I suddenly realized as her blank look deepened into one of her I Look Like I'm Here But I'm Really Not expressions. "Why did you lie to me?"

"Would you have come if I didn't have some sort of a Plan?" The challenge was vintage Francesca, but the voice couldn't quite bring it off. Too thin, too shaky. Like the speaker.

Gordon knocked back two glassfuls of whisky during our little chat. We were sitting cross-legged on the bed, and now he joined us. He really is very big. Everything sank as he settled himself next to me and wound a muscular arm around my puffy shoulders. He reeked of Scotch as he pulled me closer and kissed my ear. I pulled away quickly and he laughed.

"Behave, Gordon," Francesca warned him.

"What's happened to Nicky?" I asked.

"Who cares?" Obviously Gordon didn't.

"Well, if he killed Janine and fingered you, I'd think you'd care." My ear was still moist from his kiss. I moved away from him, a matter of inches in that confined space.

"I don't," he yawned. "He's such a jerk, always blaming me for everything when he was the one who always got us into trouble. Nobody ever suspected me. Nobody. Whining little jerk. He cried to the cops, and they believed him. Everybody believed him."

"We really have to get out of here, Crissy," Francesca pleaded with me. "It's too cold, and someone's bound to think of this place eventually. My mother probably thought it was sold when Aunt Winnie moved to Florida, if she thought about it at all."

Gordon slid off the bed. "I'm starving. I'm going to get something to eat. I hope you're into heroes stuffed with everything, Cris."

"I'm not hungry."

"Bring coffee," Francesca said. "Make sure it's scalding hot."

Gordon pulled on a fedora and pasted a thick mustache over his upper lip. He looked like a poor man's Indiana Jones. "Later," he said, and left, the din he made pounding down the stairs resonating through the barren house like the rumble of city traffic. We could even hear him double-locking the front door.

"He always does that," Francesca read my mind, going limp when the noise stopped. "We left it open for you." She tried to smile.

"Are you okay?"

She sighed. "I guess. It's been endless since we got here. It seemed such a terrific idea when I first thought of it. I mean, he was frantic! Frantic! You'd think he'd been tried, convicted, sentenced, the whole thing. And we got high, which probably wasn't too smart. My thinking under the influence is always very—dramatic. But I do think coming up with this place was a stroke of pure genius."

"It obviously worked." I hesitated. I'd been thinking a lot about this, and I had to say my piece while Gordon was out. "He *hasn't* been tried or convicted or sentenced. That's the fact of it. And if you go anywhere, to California, anywhere, cross state lines, all that, you're in big trouble, and he's in bigger."

"He can't get a fair shake here, Cris. If we do it this way, make a public point of the fact that New York is totally prejudiced against him, buy some time so that maybe—just maybe—people investigating this case will look a little harder at Nicky—"

"You're fantasizing, Francesca. You're fantasizing and running a huge risk."

She squinted at me in that dim room. It was getting darker by the second. "Are you sure you didn't tell your mother? This all sounds much more like your mother than you."

"Believe what you want. You know I'm right. You've been playing Lovers on the Lam or something, but it's beginning to wear a little thin. Am I right?"

"No."

I was.

"He's innocent, Cris."

"Not a word I would use to describe Gordon."

"You know what I mean. He didn't kill Janine Billings."

"Then he should stick around so everyone knows it. You said yourself Gordon's parents hired the best lawyer possible."

"Why did you come, if you feel this way?"

"I'm not sure. You sounded—lost. I've been a basket case about where you were and all. Maybe I just wanted to make sure you were okay. I know I hated lying to my mother."

"Don't be such a goody-goody. You lie to your mother."

"Never like this. Never so planned and deliberate. And never taking part in something as serious—"

"You're mad at Gordon because he came on to you earlier."

"I couldn't care less about that. I'm sure you two have been having a high old time in this four-poster."

It was her turn to hesitate. "He's been out of it a lot, between the booze, the pot, and his special little habit."

"Cocaine?"

"Now and then. He gets goofy. Not sexy. Definitely not sexy."

"Poor Juliet."

"You're being a pain, Crissy."

"I want you to bag this great plan of yours! Whatever it is. Talk him into giving himself up. Everything will work out."

She didn't say anything for a minute, which amazed me.

"Talk him into giving himself up."

"He won't. I can't."

"You could try."

"I have."

I was stunned.

"Everything you've just said, I've said to him. At considerable personal risk, I might add."

"What? Did he hit you?"

She laughed. "You are totally predictable, Cris! Totally predictable, naive, gullible—"

"He hit you."

No answer.

"Why don't *I* put it up to him? He won't hit me."

"Don't bet on it."

"Francesca!"

She shrugged. "It only happens when he's—out of it: high, stoned. Out of it. He's always sorry, later on."

I looked around. It was getting incredibly dark, and the prospect of staying in this deep freeze in the dark had no appeal whatsoever. I grabbed her hand, and it was like an ice cube. "Let's get out of here!"

She didn't move.

I tugged at her hand and began to back off the bed. "C'mon! Let's get out of here! If he's left on his own, he'll be forced to give himself up!"

"Cris, I can't—"

"Don't argue! We don't have time. You agree with me, you know you do. This seemed like a good idea. It wasn't. You got into all this because you got stoned and he's sexy and it seemed like a big adventure. But now you're risking serious consequences. Don't make a bad idea worse by going on with it. You're not doing either of you any favors. In fact, the only thing to do is leave him here and let him figure it out on his own. He'll be fine. He'll be in a whole lot less trouble than if you run away."

She wasn't moving quickly, but she was following me. She hadn't let go of my hand. "I can't just *leave*."

"You must just leave! If you wait for him to come back, he'll talk you out of it. Or beat you out of it."

"Don't overreact."

"He hit you. You admitted he hit you."

"Hit. Not *beat*. Big difference."

"I wouldn't know. Brian never even raises his voice."

"Brian!" She laughed. "The Bobbsey Twins: you and baby Brian."

"Beats Gordon the Glom."

She giggled. "The what?"

"Your word: glom. A glib, obtuse mediocrity."

"Hardly applicable to Gordon."

"Totally applicable." I felt like we were playing word games, as we had so often, in school and out.

There was a crash below us, and we both went rigid.

"He's back," Francesca said. She tried not to sound sorry about it.

"He'll leave again."

"Not tonight. I'm sure he's bought more than sandwiches.

He always does. Forget it. I wouldn't have gone with you anyway."

Right.

He lumbered up the stairs and was panting by the time he reached us. He dumped several small paper bags onto the bed. Francesca lunged after them, snatching them up and placing them in a neat little row on the floor. "You got coffee, right? You want to slop it all over the bed?"

"Cool it." He sounded pissed; more than pissed.

"What's wrong?"

"I think your little friend brought company."

"What are you talking about? Nobody followed me. I made sure of that."

"Yeah?"

"Gordon," Francesca soothed, "you're paranoid, you know you are. And when you're hungry, it's worse, so let's eat. This coffee feels hot, right through the bag. I'm going to keep my hands around it 'til they thaw."

He clutched a paper bag and went off with it, slumping into a pitch-black corner opposite the bed and near the door. He rattled paper, unwrapped his sandwich, and then inhaled it, chewing noisily. It was disgusting to listen to.

I sat back on the bed as Francesca wrapped her hands around her little Styrofoam cup for warmth. I looked over at the black hole where Gordon sat, devouring his food like a slobbering animal, and I felt incredibly tired.

"Why did Nicky kill her?" I asked. Nobody'd said anything for several minutes, and I was gagging listening to Gordon slurping his food.

"They had a fight, I guess." Francesca sounded weak, as though any strength she had left was draining out of her.

"Who cares?" Gordon muttered, his mouth audibly full.

"He was certainly in a violent mood," Francesca remembered. "If Brian hadn't stood up to him, who knows what he'd have done at Markie's? He might have killed someone right there in her apartment!"

"Oh, horrors!" Gordon mocked her with a squeaky high voice. "Blood all over the antiques!" I glared at him. "She probably got on his nerves." There was a thickness to his speech; his mouth was still full. "She could really get on your nerves."

I could no longer see him. He could see us because the lights from the street stretched across the bed like a wide finish-line banner. He could see us, but probably only in deep shadow.

Francesca shuddered. I put an arm around her and pulled her closer.

"Hey, you guys!" Gordon sputtered. "You getting weird on me, here? What's going on up there?"

"Don't be such a pig, Gordon." I was sick of listening to him slobber over his food.

"Who you calling 'pig'?"

"We should start thinking about getting out of here," Francesca said.

"Who you calling 'pig'!"

"Calm down."

"Don't pull this with me, Crissy." He slurred my name badly. His mouth wasn't full. He was on something. And he was losing it.

I let go of Francesca and sat very straight, staring into the black hole where he was. Then I turned slightly and reached over to the night table, where I picked up the telephone receiver.

"Who're you callin'?" he wanted to know.

"You'll need some transportation out of here. I don't think the F train is an option."

"Very funny." He didn't really think so.

"I know a car service. They'll take you out of town, no questions asked." I was dialing home. It was actually ringing. Three, four. One more and the machine would pick up.

"Hang up, Crissy. You're pissing me off."

The machine clicked on. Alex, nasal, monotone. Sweet music to my ears. "You have reached . . ." I prayed Gordon wouldn't hear the beep.

"Hang up, Crissy," Gordon mumbled. He sounded sleepy.

I watched Francesca's eyes widen as she heard the beep.

"Did you hang up?" Gordon growled. He was moving around over there. He was struggling to his feet.

Francesca leaned across me and disconnected the call.

No one said anything for a while.

"Janine asked for it," Gordon said to no one in particular.

Janine asked for it? I think I stopped breathing for a moment. I knew something more than the dark and the cold had entered that room. Someone I didn't know at all and might not have hung out with if I had known her had been killed, brutally, and left on a dark, dank, stinking subway platform. Gordon had dismissed her as if she were something disposable: garbage.

"She asked for it." Gordon repeated. His speech was thick, slurry.

"I guess we can't go tonight." Francesca tried to shift gears. Her voice was too shaky to carry it off. She rubbed her upper arms rapidly. "Another night in Siberia. I shall never be warm again."

"Francesca—" We had to get out of here.

"We made up a song about her, Nicky and me. We made up a song about Janine." Gordon was really into it now.

"Good for you and Nicky." Francesca sounded sick of it all. Despite the tremor in her voice, she was almost too tired to care anymore.

"You're so smart!" He was furious. "You and your friend there, smarter than anyone. Better than anyone. Know it *all*." He began to curse.

"Sing your song for us, Gordon." Maybe it would distract him. Maybe he'd sing himself to sleep. I had to deflect his rage somehow.

"I need to plan," Francesca whispered to me. "Help me plan, Crissy. I can't think straight."

" 'Janine Billings,' " Gordon warbled, way off key. " 'She's always willing/To do whatever we ask/On her back, on her face/In a cab or at her place/She's always up to the task!' " He hiccuped, then belched loudly.

"If you're going to puke, get into the bathroom!" Francesca railed at him, an ugly memory displacing fear briefly. "I mean it, Gordon! I am not going to clean up after you again!"

I won't tell you what he said then. He began humming his hideous little song. I slid off the bed. "I'm outta here."

It was as if the walls moved, the way he came out of the blackness, his size, his bulk rushing at me. He grabbed me, and even through the padding my coat provided, I could feel the steel clamp of his grip.

"Gordon!" Francesca screamed.

"You're not going anywhere."

"Let go of me!" It was supposed to be sharp, but it came out squeaky scared, because I was.

He held on to me, tightening his grip. "What am I supposed to do? Let you wander off? Wave bye-bye? See you around and call me when you get there? You guys really think I'm stupid. Or maybe you just think I'm out of it, tripping a little? Forget it! *Forget it!*" He shoved me toward the bed, but I fell, hit the hard-wood sideboard, and bounced to the floor in a heap.

I started to get up, but he was standing right over me. I was pinned against the bed's sideboard with my head pushed forward by the mattress, which overhung the sideboard by a few inches. "Move, Gordon."

"Stay there. Just stay right there."

If fear is a sudden sense of cold and dread, when your mouth goes dry and every nerve ending stands at attention, that was my reaction to Gordon Larrimer at that moment. I felt trapped and threatened, claustrophic and panicky. I wanted to scream and scream and scream, and when I finally stopped, I wanted to wake up in my bed at home as if this had been the worst of all possible nightmares.

I stared at the floor because looking down was all I could manage easily, and I kept perfectly, noiselessly still. There was a desperate struggle going on above me—Francesca shrieking and flailing at Gordon—but it only made things tougher for me, because Gordon was moving around so unpredictably. I pulled my legs as far under me as I could manage and crouched against the bed, trying not to get stepped on.

Francesca's screaming quickly changed to crying, and suddenly they had both moved away from me. I scrambled to my feet. Gordon was slapping her, knocking her across the room with one blow after another, and she moved away from him with her arms raised over her face to protect herself.

"Stop it!" I dove after him, but it was like hitting a brick wall, punching his massive back.

He turned his head, like he couldn't believe I was really coming on. He laughed at me. And then he slapped me, a tremendous blow across my face with his open palm. I staggered back and fell across the soft pile on top of the bed. My face was hot and stinging from the blow, and I felt lightheaded, not quite steady or able to get back onto my feet. By the time I rallied a little, he had hold of Francesca, and he threw her onto the bed beside me like he was piling up debris in an attic. He definitely did not care how or in what shape she landed.

Francesca turned away from me, folding herself up slowly, pulling her legs up off the floor and tucking them under her. She was sobbing quietly.

Gordon slumped onto the floor against the opposite wall and spewed curses. Kids curse a lot, and for a lot of reasons. We think it's cool, it pisses off our parents, it shocks some people. We don't even hear ourselves after a while, it becomes so reflex. But what Gordon was saying was cursing at its worst. It was sinister, intimidating, scary.

No one said anything then. Francesca's sobbing ebbed into silence, although I could see her shoulders heave. She sat facing away from me, curled into a tight crouch, her head way down. I watched Gordon—what I could see of him—and I watched her, and no one said anything for what seemed like hours.

It's amazing how you can turn your mind off. I refused to think about anything: what was happening, what was going to happen, how to cope with it all. As if thinking might make a noise. As if thinking might somehow stir Gordon, the sleeping giant. The sleeping, murderous giant.

I refused to think about what to do next. What could I do? What would he do?

What had he already done?

Everything. . . . I could hear someone screaming, down on the street, a woman screaming, and I remembered Janine at Markie's party: screaming and screaming. Nobody listened. We all heard her, we all had to hear her, but nobody listened.

"What was that?" Gordon asked suddenly.

It startled Francesca and me, made us both jump slightly.

"What was *that*?"

"Someone's screaming," I said.

"Not *that*." He was in a rage, but something had punctured it. He was scared as well.

"I didn't hear anything else," I said. *I wish I'd heard something else.*

"Shut up!" He got up and moved quickly toward the windows, standing to one side to look out onto the street. He flattened himself against the wall to get a better look.

I grabbed Francesca's hand. It was still like an ice cube. I pulled her after me off the bed. We tiptoed toward the hallway, hand in hand. I couldn't believe how cold her hand was right through my wool glove.

We got to the hallway, which was pitch-black, but we never slowed down. We didn't have to see to know our way in this house. I pushed her ahead of me down the stairs. I was right behind her, and the stairs creaked so loudly, I winced and turned my head expecting Gordon to be right behind us. She began to run. I slid over a couple of steps and nearly fell but kept going, right behind her, my mouth dry and wide open.

He grabbed my coat. I never heard him behind me, and when I felt the first tug, I thought it had caught on something, so I tugged back to pull free. He laughed as though we were playing a game, and yanked so hard on my coat, I fell, sprawled all over the top few steps of the final flight leading to the street. Francesca had already opened the front door when she realized I wasn't right behind her. She stood there, silhouetted by the lights from the street, looking up the stairs as Gordon reeled me in like a fish. She started to back up, and I bellowed. I mean, I never knew I could make that much noise.

"Go! Go on! Get help! Go on!"

"She's dead if you walk out that door," Gordon said, as mildly as if he'd been talking about the weather.

Francesca froze where she stood.

"Shut the door, baby." Gordon slid into his old smooth-as-silk self.

"No, Francesca! *Go!*"

He pulled my hair so hard, I thought my head would snap right off my neck.

She closed the door, and we were in complete darkness. She began to climb the stairs with a slow, measured, defeated step, and Gordon put his arms under mine and pulled me to my feet. My scalp was burning with pain, and tears streamed down my face. I wasn't even aware I was crying until the first salty drips splashed into my mouth.

I couldn't believe we were going back into that room. Gordon shoved me onto the bed, and when Francesca came in, he slammed the door to the hall behind her. She slid next to me and pulled me against her.

"I'm sorry," she said. "I'm so sorry." She touched my hair and I started to bawl.

"Give me the money," Gordon told her. His voice was as hard as stone.

I pulled back and watched her dig into her pockets for wads of cash.

"All of it!" he barked.

She sniffed back tears and took off her right shoe. She had another stash in the heel.

He counted it, several times. "Forty, sixty, two hundred . . . forty, sixty, eighty, three hundred . . . " He counted out eight hundred dollars. Then he stuffed it all in his pants pocket. He looked at me and held out his hand. "Now you."

I dug into my deep coat pocket and handed over my cash. "You can leave us here, Gordon." I was talking, but it was like listening to someone else, someone calm, together. "Rip out the phone and lock us in. We won't budge 'til tomorrow, and you can be halfway to—anywhere—by then."

I couldn't believe me. No tears, no quivering or crying or quaking. I felt numb. My tears had dried. I was all trembled out. But I didn't want to think about what was coming next.

Because I knew what was coming next.

In the movies, when the story involves murder, suspense, the wrap-up, things always spin out fast. Forget it. I mean, I'd found Francesca, we now knew who'd really killed Janine Billings, and everything had come to a complete halt. Nobody said anything. Nobody moved very much. We all watched each other. And waited.

And waited.

It crossed my mind that we might freeze to death there, and how grotesque would it be when someone finally found us, clued in by the inevitable stench of our decaying corpses in the late spring or early summer. I could almost write the headline:

TEEN KILLER FOUND DEAD WITH TWO GIRLFRIENDS

or

**FUGITIVE MURDERER AND ACCOMPLICES SHARE
FINAL DEEP FREEZE**

"Gordon?" My voice was the first sound in what seemed like hours.

"What?" Hostile. Suspicious. Wide-awake.

"What are you going to do?"

"You really want to know?"

"Are you waiting for daylight? Give us a clue."

"I don't know yet."

I couldn't believe I was talking about it. Like we were making plans for the evening. Like we had resigned ourselves to the inevitability of it. Like we didn't care.

"Can I ask you something?"

"What?" Slightly less hostile. Very slightly.

"Why did you kill Janine? She meant nothing to you."

"She wanted more than her share of the take from Markie's. She wanted that ring, dammit. That ring was worth more than all the rest of it, even the cash. And she wanted to *wear* it. Stupid . . ."

"You and Nicky couldn't keep it from her?"

"She never laid a hand on it, but she started to scream about how she was going to the police, how she was going to tell them about that heist and all the others."

"Where was Nicky?"

"He took off. He was feeling lousy. He'd been drinking and tripping all day. He was sick as a dog by then. He knew I could handle it."

"Why the subway?"

He shrugged. "It was there. I shoved her down the stairs. I was trying to scare her. But she just got louder. She had a voice that went right through you. Nicky let her tag along. It was never my idea. She got on my nerves."

I knew better, but I had to ask him. "How could you?" All I could think of was what Brian had said to me: *Whoever killed her nearly cut her head off.* "How *could* you?"

He made a sort of guttural noise, like he was clearing his throat. I thought for an instant he might be getting emotional, show some remorse even, but then he laughed. He actually laughed.

"I didn't know," Francesca said quietly. "Honestly, I guess I knew he could have done it, but I couldn't deal. I would never—"

"I know," I said. I did.

The phone rang. We all jumped like the room had been electrically charged and plugged directly into each of us. It rang and rang and rang.

"Don't even think about it," Gordon said.

"Probably a wrong number," Francesca muttered.

"Maybe not," I hoped. I was too wired to be wimpy anymore. I wasn't going to crawl around someone as slimy as Gordon Larrimer. "How come the phone's still turned on? The heat's off, the electric—"

"I'm not sure," Francesca said.

"Maybe it's the police," I taunted him. "Or my mother. Or Francesca's mother. Maybe somebody finally remembered this place, remembered how much Francesca hung out here. It's probably the police."

"Shut up!"

We did, nodding at one another in the darkness we'd become so used to. It would be more effective to let him think about it now. Stop talking and let him think about it. It wasn't something he was very skilled at.

I was certainly thinking. My brain had been essentially off for hours. It kicked back into working order. There had to be a way out of here.

The phone began to ring again. It was a shocking sound in this cold, dark room where fear had been as thick as the shadows and was still very much a presence, if not quite so paralyzing as before.

Ring. Ring. Ring. Ring. Ring. Ring. Ring.

"Definitely not a wrong number," I said.

"I think I'll knock you off first, Crissy. You're getting on my nerves."

"What did you use on Janine? A Swiss Army knife? Something imported and expensive."

"Cris—" Francesca put a restraining hand on my arm.

"A Swiss Army knife? That's for Boy Scouts. Want to see the knife, Crissy? I have it on me," Gordon boasted.

"That's okay." Maybe I was overdoing it.

"I'd be glad to show it to you." He warmed to the idea, pulling himself up from his spot near the windows. He had to be stiff, he'd been there so long, and he took a minute to stretch and flex.

He's lazy, I suddenly realized. He has never played any sports; he hates sports, in fact, and he doesn't jog or do anything physical. He smokes, drinks, does drugs, and lounges around. He's probably in lousy shape for someone his age.

He began to look like a lump of Jell-O to me, standing there in the half-light from the windows. Then I remembered how it felt to hit against him. Like a brick wall. And how easily he had hauled me back up here. Like I weighed a lot less than I actually do.

Cool it. Slow down. Chill out. He's tough, he's strong, and he's already killed someone.

Janine Billings.

"Whoever killed her nearly cut her head off." Brian had been blown away by that.

Brian. I missed him incredibly at that moment.

Gordon didn't come over to show me his knife. He glanced out the window, and something kept him there and made him flatten himself against the wall.

Please . . . someone be there . . . someone help us. . . .

I began to look around, always keeping a close check on Gordon. This four-poster bed was big, the biggest thing in the room. The footboard was a broad, sculpted piece of mahogany with a large globelike decoration rising from its center. I focused on that. It looked like a bowling ball with accents. I kept glancing sideways at Gordon as I leaned forward, twisted the globelike piece, and almost lost it as it moved and then pulled free. Francesca was watching my every move, her eyes widening as I balanced the big, solid globe in my hands. It had ridges; it was shaped like a pineapple, I realized. But it was solid mahogany, like the bed frame. Heavy. Lethal, I hoped.

I slid it under the pile of covers on the bed. Now I was watching Gordon exclusively. So was Francesca, only she was trembling so violently, I could feel it from where I sat.

Maybe he sensed us looking at him, because he turned toward us suddenly. Something had changed about him, hardened. He reached the bed in a couple of strides. And he pulled something from his pants pocket, something small that quickly became larger and flashed in the shaft of light from the street.

He grabbed Francesca and pulled her off the bed, and I dropped the mahogany ball. It rolled uselessly away and thudded to the floor. It even sounded like a bowling ball.

I screeched like a banshee, stood up on the bed, and pulled the top covering up with me: a woven rug with fringe at either end. I pitched myself directly onto Gordon, covering him completely with the rug and falling on top of the rug *and* Gordon. We both fell to the floor. I kept screaming, but it was a war cry now. I scrambled up and grabbed Francesca and we raced to the bedroom door, hand in hand. Gordon was on his feet as well, but I think he was still struggling to pull free of the rug. I couldn't tell you. I didn't look around.

I also don't remember stepping on a single stair. My legs felt like ramrod-stiff steel weights, but we got to the bottom in complete darkness and record time. I stumbled on the stone steps to the street and fell, scraping both knees so that they bled. We were on Sixth Avenue before we realized we were still running hand in hand. Francesca was headed right under the wheels of a truck, but I yanked her back.

And it was then the police caught up with us.

Gordon was right, as it turned out. No one had actually followed me to Cornelia Street, but when I dialed home and got our answering machine, the caller-ID box attached to our phone registered Aunt Winnie's phone number. The police had installed a high-tech caller-ID system for us right after Francesca disappeared, one they were able to monitor constantly. They'd picked up the Cornelia Street phone number after Francesca's initial call, but figured it was of no significance since the number turned up listed under the shopkeeper's name. When it showed up again after my call, they dug a little deeper and immediately knew they were on to something since Aunt Winnie's name surfaced as the owner of the house. Then they contacted Francesca's mother to verify her connection to Aunt Winnie—she was mortified not to have thought of Cornelia Street before.

"I honestly assumed she'd sold it," was what she told the police detective. When she repeated the story to my mother, she added, "Aunt Winnie and I never really got along."

"How come Aunt Winnie's telephone's the same as the shop's?" I asked my father. I knew he'd know. I knew he'd questioned the detectives on the case relentlessly about every little detail.

"Apparently it's always been set up like that. She rarely used the phone during the day, and the shop's shut at night, so it was economical and convenient; and since the shop's still going, nobody ever needed to change it." He was so glad I'd asked.

"Thank heaven you tried calling home," Mom said. "But you knew Gordon would never let you talk to anyone."

"I just did it." I did. I dialed home almost without thinking. "Maybe I was hoping you'd hear background noise, or something. I forgot all about the caller-ID box. You know me, Mom: I *always* call home."

Inside joke, totally true when I was younger, but not lately. Maybe I had more sense when I was younger. I'll have to rethink that.

The police were the ones trying to reach us on the phone, and they were organizing a hostage task force when Francesca and I ran out the front door and right past them.

My mother's Structure is history. She's mellowed big time about mealtimes and schedules and life in general. She's always busy, but she'll drop whatever she's doing if any of us need to talk. She's writing a book about parenting, with the emphasis on how to deal with teenagers. She's excited because she thinks parents tend to minimize their effectiveness once their kids start to sound smarter than they really are. She's also been approached by some TV producers to be on a talk show, but she's told them no way. Fischer Brocknaw now lists her on his stationery letterhead as a "consultant." She must have told him he could do that, because her name is up there, right under his and some of his top people's.

I've babbled on incessantly about Mom and how incredible everyone thinks she is, but I'm finally realizing it myself. She *is* incredible, Dad is incredible, Alex is incredible; Mark too. I'm not sure how I lucked out to be a part of this family, but I'm grateful for it.

Alan Gelber wants to do a follow-up segment for *Weekend Closeup*, but no thanks. He's asked Neva out, and she'd go, but her mom's put the lid on it.

Markie's going away to boarding school next year after all. Her father said she could invite a group of us to spend the week of spring break at their palace on Lyford Cay in the Bahamas to sort of soften the devastating blow of leaving our class, but my parents don't want me to go. They feel the press would climb all over us for partying so spectactularly before Gordon is even tried for Janine's murder. I've always wanted to visit Markie's palace on Lyford Cay—she's come back from there tanned and full of incredible beach stories for years—but going now doesn't really appeal to me all that much.

Mrs. Walpole actually stood up in front of us in college lab the other day and "recommended" we include something about all this on our college applications. "Only if you were actively involved," she added. That's *sick*.

I don't go anywhere. I mean, leaving my bedroom is a big deal these days. Brian's here a lot, but I'm such a drag, I'm afraid he's going to get sick of me. He spends more time playing computer games with Mark than he does with me, but I know he's trying his best to wait out this phase I'm going through. All I really want to do is sleep, yet when I do sleep, I have fierce, terrible nightmares. I don't remember any details when I wake up, usually in a cold sweat, but Janine's always on my mind, Janine and that cold, claustrophobic little bedroom at Aunt Winnie's. That room got so *dark*, like the lonely tunnel end of a subway platform.

Francesca and I haven't spoken, but our mothers have. They've even progressed to calling each other by their first names.

I read and reread the letter from Janine's mother. I could recite it, I've read it so many times. And I've been thinking: We all trashed Janine without knowing her. We passed around those kinky rumors and never worried about this being an actual person we were talking about. If we'd thought about it, if we'd given a single unbiased thought to *her*, maybe we'd have slowed it down some. We should have wondered why she let people use her apartment. We should have wondered what her life was like.

Janine had no friends, her mother wrote. No friends. No Neva, Markie, Ellie, Leslie. Brian. Francesca. Every time I read it, I feel lonelier. Why didn't I react when she started screaming at Markie's party? How could I ignore her like that, be annoyed at the *noise* she was making? How can we live together on this planet and not care about one another?

I knew someone had walked into my room, but I assumed it was my mother, checking back to see if I was smoking. Or sleeping. All this sleeping is making her crazy, but she doesn't bug me about it. Or anything. Not yet.

When Francesca said "Hi," I nearly tore Janine's mother's letter in half. I jumped off my bed. She looked thin and pale, and her hair was its real color (I think). She had on jeans and a really normal-looking bulky sweater. I might have had trouble recognizing her if I didn't know her so well, but there is still only one Francesca.

"*Hi!* Come in. Sit. How are you?"

She slid onto the foot of my bed. "How are you?"

"Pretty gross, I think. I last showered a couple of days ago."

"There's not much point to anything, is there?"

I didn't know what to say.

She looked up at me. She kept sliding her hand over my comforter as though she could smooth away the quilting. I sat down on the other side of the bed and leaned toward her.

"My father actually phoned me yesterday." She caught my slightly wary reaction immediately. "No, seriously. He did. He had to introduce himself, of course. It's been a long time between phone calls."

"What did he say?"

She shrugged. "Not much. He avoided asking any direct questions. I'm sure he'd gotten all the answers he wanted from my mother. It was a short call. We basically have nothing to say to one another. He did ask—"

"What?"

She managed a half smile. "Where I'm going to college."

"Really. What'd you say?"

She focused on my comforter. "You know how I feel about college."

She had made up her mind to go, after all, and we both knew it. I've been doing a little thinking about college. Alex is so psyched to be going to Yale; Mark is ready to fill out his own application, right this minute; Brian's hoping for Tulane. He'll probably make it. I wonder where we'll all be a year from now.

Wherever we are, we won't be the same people we were before Markie's party. Nothing will ever be as simple, as possible, as carefree. As guilt free.

But one thing is sure: Mom will be here. And Daddy. His best Christmas present to us was announcing he'd turned down all the foreign job offers.

"We can't ever move," he said. "What would your grandmother do without us?"

Which got a big laugh, of course, the biggest from Gram, the world's most independent person.

"They said on CNN this morning they're setting a trial date," Francesca murmured. She was looking straight at me, and her eyes said, *Help!*

I hope they have Gordon chained, hand and foot, in some airless little hole. In one of my worst nightmares, we are back at Aunt Winnie's, and he is wielding an axe, and Francesca is in pieces, and the stairs lead to nowhere.

"My mother seems to be keeping close tabs on everything," Francesca went on, moving away from her fear, shedding that too-tight skin as only she can. "She says I'll be called on to testify. You too, Crissy. And of course, they've kept close tabs on Nicky Baylor. He's made some sort of deal, I hear, but he still has to be held accountable for all those things he stole!" She set her jaw. "Gordon probably thinks I won't say much. He's in for a big surprise. I'm going to tell them everything. *Every*thing."

"That's great." Never before had I had any trouble talking to Francesca. I couldn't think of anything to say. Finally I asked her, "Where will you apply? College, I mean."

That sort of startled her, but she shrugged it off. "NYU, maybe. Their film school is supposed to be amazing."

"Makes sense." I was still clutching Janine's mother's letter, and I made a move to put it on my night table when something prompted me to hand it to her instead.

"What's this?"

"Read it."

It seemed like hours passed, and I began to wonder whether she was reading it or just staring at it. Finally she looked up at me and her eyes were brimming, so I knew she'd read it. "I thought we might try to get up a scholarship fund. In her name. In her memory. She didn't have much of a life. People should at least remember." I have no idea where all that came from. I guess I'm my mother's daughter.

She didn't move for a minute. Then tentatively, clumsily, Francesca leaned over and hugged me. I hugged her back and realized this was what she had come for, this was what she needed, whether she had known it or not. Janine had no friends, but Francesca and I had always had each other. Would always have each other.

Sort of.

It would never be the same for us. I knew that too. Things had shifted. Francesca's star status had mellowed into something more ordinary. I no longer stood in her shadow, the wannabe, the fan.

We were moving on.

A note about the author

Jane Sughrue Giberga was born in New York City, and attended a private girls' high school there. The daughter of a journalist, she has been writing for most of her life. In addition, she has worked for the three major TV networks, managed the offices of a women's club and a community center, and raised three children. At present she is devoting herself to writing full-time. She enjoys reading, music, theater, movies, and—yes—dinners with her family. Mrs. Giberga resides with her husband in Forest Hills, New York.

Acknowledgments

There are a number of people who provided me with constant encouragement and unwavering faith.
A very special thanks to Philip Spitzer, my agent, and Michèle Foley, my editor. And without my wonderful sister, Sue Carrington, and my dear friend Anne-Lise Spitzer, there might never have been *Friends to die for*.
—J.S.G.